1

Harrison: A boy deathly infatuated with a temptress

Emily: A mental girl trying to get better

August: The girl everyone loves, but no one knows

Jason: The bullshit boy

Kennedy: The girl who knows too much

Five teens, just trying to learn the art of being here.

The Art of Being Here

by pluto

The Art of Being Here

Published by Lulu

Originally Published in the United States by Lulu Press in 2016.

Cover design by:

Michael Howard
http://www.nvm-illustration.co.uk

ISBN 978-1-329-81598-8

Dedication

To the humans who need to learn the art of being here --

I'm still learning too.

To my family, friends, other fellow planets, and lost souls.

I love you, and thank you

p.

Harrison

Her name was August and the only thing I can remotely remember about her is absolutely everything.

She was all things beautiful. Her eyes reminded me of a soft flower petal, and her smile reminded me of a lost memory slowly found. She was every good feeling in the world. To explain her in words is not close to what you felt when she looked at you.

The first time she looked at me was when I was in third grade. She just moved from Vermont, and I swear you could still see the snowflakes in her hair. I had the honor or curse of having her in Mrs. Jones's class in 15E. She walked into the room with such ease I almost didn't realize the big bang she triggered. It wasn't just me that felt it; the whole class experienced the same. She was like a rare flower, or a new discovered universe.

She had to stand in front of the class in her blue dress and introduce herself. Her name flew off her tongue and landed into my hands. I was so scared that I almost dropped it, but I held it dearly. As if on queue, she locked eyes with me and I knew I was fucked. Can you imagine? A third grader already feeling fucked? I didn't even realize it until it was too late. I was entranced by her, complete captivated, and I loved it. She smiled at me, knowing that I was already at her feet. Mrs. Jones told her to take a seat, and she picked one next to Emily and Jason in the front row. Two rows in front of me.

I still cannot decide if I was resurrected that day or murdered. But either or, I was hers. I was completely hers.

✪

Eight years passed and I'm still hers, and she still knows. I have succumbed to a normal boy on the soccer team, and she has risen to the almighty. She was already there anyway. Every year I seemed to have her in at least one class, and this year is no different.

She has grown up exactly how I pictured it. Shadows following her everywhere she went as if she was the sun itself. Everyone loved her, as they should. Her boyfriend, Kevin, notices this too but he is not worried. He knows that he has her, except he is utterly wrong. It is she that has him. It is she that has the whole world in the middle of her palm. Her soft eyes and harmonious laugh does not fool me. She knows the secrets of the world and she is so very good at hiding them.

Temptress. Siren. Devil. Angel. Whichever she is, August knows too much. Many underestimate her, and that is their own mistake. As for me, an enamored, tall, normal and boring boy, I know the truth. And she knows I do.

It was in the library when she confronted me. It was after school and my shift at the schools's library was nearing to an end. I was tiredly stacking books back into their order, when she appeared.

"Harrison, is it?" Her voice entered my lungs and restricted me from saying anything. I nodded like the dumb fuck I was. "I was looking for a book. My personal reading project is coming up and I haven't even started. Do you have any recommendations for someone who doesn't read for fun?" She smiled that devil smile of hers, and didn't even have to push me to do as told.

"Salinger is always a good read, as well as Bukowski," My voice was hoarse, and I caught a glimmer of a smirk tugging on her lips. She knew she had me, she always knew.

"Which one is your favorite?" She asked, looking at the books that I have stacked.

"Salinger if I'm feeling nostalgic, and Bukowski if I need... well anything," I responded trying to look anywhere but her eyes.

"Bukowski then," She smiled and I was a goner.

Emily

The strawberries that made a smile on my pancakes were mocking me. Even pancakes can be happier than me. In rebellion, I pushed the pancakes off my table and waited until someone rushed in wondering what the crash was.

Two nurses came bursting through the door and immediately scowled from seeing my position. I had my arms folded and a casual frown on. One nurse angrily whispered to the other, and then stomped out of the room. I liked seeing nurses angry; I liked seeing people as angry as I am.

"If you didn't like your food, you could have just asked us to exchange it for something else," Sammy, a new intern nurse, said as she started to pick up my mess.

"It's not that I didn't like my food. I didn't like the strawberries in that pattern," I responded. Sammy sighed and threw away the mess into the garbage.

"If you didn't like the strawberries, you could've just moved them aside," She retorted.

"That's boring," She sighed again, and walked out the room probably getting another breakfast for me.

I tried to itch the tape on my skin holding the band in place.

I hate Tuesdays.

I played with the strings coming undone on the blanket my Nana made me. I can't ask her to sew it back anymore. I would ask my parents to get it fixed but they don't come by anymore. No one does.

"Here," Sammy walked in with a new tray, "and if you don't like it, then just don't eat it," She placed it down forcefully on my table. Scrambled eggs and toast filled the paper plate in the saddest fashion. So I began to eat it.

The scene outside my window seemed like a tragedy, and the T.V was stuck on some Spanish drama. I think the main characters dad just died.

This was a normal Tuesday for me. Get my medicine first thing in the morning while I have a sad plate a breakfast on a sad day with a sad channel playing in this sad room with sad little old me. Sad Tuesdays.

Sad Tuesday's are also Visitor day which also dims my mood even more. My last visitor was some girl from my French class. I never talked to her in my life, but she still came. And I still pushed her away. That was two months ago. No one comes now.

I stared at the ceiling, silently thanking the sobs of the insane Spanish main character to keep me from my thoughts.

I hated this place. It smelt like old fish sticks and it was nothing like the movies. When you see a mental ward in a hospital on T.V its pretty and rich. Usually the girl finds a boy as fucked up as she is and they slowly fall in love while healing each other.

Well, TV got it all wrong. You are all alone here while your parents hate you back home for the abundance of mental bills they have to pay. Also the only guys here are twice as fucked up as you and just simply don't give a care. Also, you can't even speak to other people in general if you received three tallies.

If you get three tallies you aren't allowed in the Main Hall for three days. Seems fair, except its not. I received three tallies for three things I didn't do.

Tally One: Having a minor breakdown in the Main Hall.

Okay, this one was my fault. But give me the benefit of the doubt. It was my first week here and when have you ever heard of a mental patient who didn't have a minor break down in their first week in a mental institution? Especially when that patient is a sad teenage girl.

Tally Two: Starting a food fight in the Common Room

This one wasn't my fault. It was some borderline bitch from the adult ward. She had an episode and starting throwing food everywhere. Which of course, made everyone else start to throw food as well. Then there you go, an old fashion food fight with mental freaks. Yet, when it was down to track the culprit all fingers pointed to me. I was completely framed. I mean, I did throw food, but who wouldn't?

Tally Three: Punching another patient in the jaw.

She had it coming.

Either way, Hell is better than this place. Therapy is a joke. The people are just as, or twice as crazy as you are. And the food here might as well be cardboard.

Hell is definitely better than this. Trust me, I've been there.

August

You can tell when someone is in love with you. Only if you look close enough, though. I am an expert already. I can tell exactly who is in love with me. Kevin, my boyfriend is head over heels. My teachers are charmed. My classmates are in awe. And Harrison Grander is off the cliff, over the moon, all the way around the Earth and twice again in love with me.

He doesn't make it obvious to contrary belief. He is outgoing and intelligent. He is athletic and honestly the perfect boy to bring home to your parents. He is the number one trophy husband. And I know he wants me to be his number one trophy wife. But I'm not number one, and I am not a trophy. Hell, not even a wife. I never will be.

I find it cute, really. How he feels is completely flattering to me, and you'd think he would seem like a cliche falling-in-love-boy, but Harrison is anything but. I can tell that when he grows up he will be more successful than anyone in our town. Too bad he is deathly infatuated with me.

It killed me seeing him so lost and lustful. So, I decided to ward him away. Someone as pure as him doesn't need someone like me, no matter how much he wants me. He doesn't, for any circumstances, need me. I decided that I'm going to make him hate me for his own good.

My plan was simple. Seduce, Conquer, and Destroy. It was the same plan every cunning, gorgeous woman acted upon to attain power. Three simple steps and Harrison Grander would have his life back.

Phase One: Seduce. This would be the easiest of the steps. So easy that I could just say his name and I would have him on the floor, begging. I began on his own

14

territory: the library. As intellectual and literate as he is, Harrison still would move continents for me. How pitiful.

I saw him stacking away books and found my opening.

"Harrison, is it?" I could see his body stiff as I spoke clearly. He turned to look at me, only able to nod his head. His golden, brown eyes were ignited at the very sight of me. This was too easy. "I was looking for a book. My personal reading project is coming up and I haven't even started. Do you have any recommendations for someone who doesn't read for fun?" I smiled my sweetest smile at him. It faltered only a nanosecond when I saw the look he gave me. I never seen anyone look at me like he did that very moment. He looked at me as if I was the very thing making him stay on this earth. He looked at me like I was the sun itself. He looked as if his body, soul, and mind was mine. He looked unbelievably, devastatingly, in complete enamor. This was much worse than I thought. He composed himself well though.

"Salinger is always a good read, as well as Bukowski," His voice was hoarse and I kind of liked it. I let my smirk show on my face and scrutinize the books he stacked.

"Which one is your favorite?" I asked reading the titles of the books on the shelf. I knew most of them- I lied when I said I didn't read for fun.

"Salinger if I'm feeling nostalgic, and Bukowski if I need... well anything," His voice was filled with unease, but immense pride in his choice of authors. I adored Bukowski, and Salinger was definitely a close second.

"Bukowski then," I replied easily, flashing him one of my brightest smile. His eyes widened in awe, and I knew I already won.

Jason

I watched all of them like ants. All of their movements were completely predictable. Every word out of their mouths could be deduced. It was so boring; I was so bored. The routine was drilled into everyone's mind and became a natural habit. They didn't even know they were stuck. It was always the same:

Wake up. Get Ready. Eat breakfast. Go to school. Talk about what you watched last night. Complain about this homework. Complain about this teacher. Talk about how cute he/she looks today. Talk about how much a dick/bitch he/she is. Go to class. Decide if you care or not. Make fun of anyone who does something, or says something abnormal. Go to lunch. Eat what they have today or decide not too. Talk about everyone you see. Talk about bullshit and bullshit and some more bullshit until you're full. Go to the bathroom. Fix whatever you need to. Go to class. Sit and listen or decide not too. End school day. Either stay after for some sport practice/game or hang out with friends at the same fucking place you always hang out. Talk about more bullshit until you are bursting from the seams. Go home. Fight with your parents or don't talk to them at all. Do your homework or watch some TV and forget about your homework. If its a Friday you either will hang out with your boyfriend or girlfriend. Not that you love them or anything drastic like that, but just because you want to feel something; anything. Go home. Get ready for bed. Sleep. Wake up the next day. Repeat.

Its a rough draft but I think if I stay scrutinizing the way ants work I can really make it perfect. The sun rises and the sun sets with no promises, or with promises we just can't understand yet.

The really funny thing was that I was one of those ants. Getting up and repeating, bursting with bullshit. But then one day, I woke up choking on how much bullshit I ate from the night before. I realized that I didn't like the taste and how I felt. So, like some sudden diet most depressed middle aged mothers start, I stopped eating bullshit. To say my eyes opened is an understatement. I feel like I was seeing and hearing for the first time.

However, everything made me want to throw up. All the bullshit everyone was eating and feeding each other was fucking revolting. You could literally see the bullshit foaming from everyone's mouth. Yet, when I tried to make it evident to others they looked at me like I was crazy. They were so far gone in their bullshit that they just couldn't believe anything other than bullshit. My best friend was so far gone the only thing I could do was leave.

So now all I do is sit and watch these ants slowly drown in their bullshit, hoping that someone would wake up choking on all their bullshit and realize that they didn't want it anymore. I waited for a year until someone finally woke up.

I was sitting on my usual curb, looking at everyone eat bullshit during lunch when a body sat itself down next to me.

"Do you want some?" she asked, shoving a bag of chips into my face. Chips were bullshit food, so I politely declined. I saw her smile from my peripheral vision. She then suddenly threw the bag of chips somewhere into the grass behind us. "Good, now I know you're the real thing." I turned to look at her fish a thermos out of her bag and show it to me. "Its soup. Homemade. I asked my mom to make it this morning." Instead of asking me this time, she unscrewed the top and poured the steaming soup into the cap. She took out an extra plastic cup from her bag and poured soup into that too. She handed me the cup and I took it not knowing what else to do. "Cheers," she smiled as she lightly tapped her cup with mine. She slowly blew on the soup, until she brought it to her pink lips. I followed suit, feeling the warmth of the tomato basil soup flow down my throat with ease.

"Do I know you?" I asked.

"No, but I know you," She replied looking at the bullshit ants.

"Really?" I edged on. She nodded her head and smiled.

"You're the bullshit boy. A lot of people warned me about you. Except, that just made me want to know you even more," She tapped her nails on her cup to an unknown beat.

"Why?" I asked. She took a deep breath before answering.

"I saw what you mean. I realized the complete bullshit everyone was spitting out. I realized I didn't care about what she wore, or who hooked up with who, or who got pregnant, or all of that shit. Because…why does that matter? There's so much more than this town and these people obsessed with themselves. I mean — there is a whole world out there. Why don't we talk about what's happening in the world and what we can do to help? Or how to help out our country before we help others? Or anything bigger than what teacher has a hairy back or who is *bangable*. I want to talk about something that matters. I want to do something that matters." She took a sip of her soup and turned to me, waiting for my response.

"I'm Jason," I smiled broadly.

"Kennedy."

Kennedy

I don't know if we all are destined for failure or greatness, but either way we are going out in the best way possible. Harrison told me I was being too optimistic, but he's the one who loves a girl who doesn't know what real love is. I have some-what faith in them though. Harrison is good at doing things most people wouldn't. (The good kind at least). Even when we were little he always surprised people. In fact, Harrison would stick with you through thick and thin unless you leave him first. Everyone loves him for that. I know this because one, I live with him, and two, I notice things.

Look, I know everyone says that they notice things most don't to seem mysterious or prove that they are *'not like most people'*, but that's what I'm here for. I'm not some loner like Jason, hating everything in the world, but that doesn't mean I don't see things. I talk when I need to, and I listen when I want — which is most of the time. I notice when people are actually being serious but cover it up by making jokes. I notice how many people hate themselves but push it off as a mechanism to make friends. I notice that everyone has something to say, and most of the time it makes sense. All you have to do is ask. Yet, people these days are afraid of doing just that.

That is why I started talking to Jason. I knew him before because he was Harrison's best friend until he left him. I always wondered what Harrison meant when he came home from school that day saying that Jason and him aren't talking anymore. He just told me that, "Jason thinks I have too much bullshit, and he doesn't want to be around that."

I never officially met Jason. Partly because I didn't want to, and well... because Harrison didn't want me to. Though, now that Harrison is completely submerged with the idea of August, I thought I could have my chance.

The bullshit boy sparked my interest the moment I looked at him. He just sat on the roadside curb, staring hatefully at everyone eating lunch in the courtyard. I could practically hear him muttering *bullshitters*.

It was amazing.

I pictured how I would meet him and how it would go down, and honestly, it concluded better than I thought. I couldn't even explain the shock on his face after I told him that I agree with him. It's like he saw the sun rise for the first time after nights he thought would never end. I was surprised he didn't recognize me as Harrison's sister, but he seemed focused on other things. After his apparent epiphany, he gave me this smile. Now, I've seen a lot of smiles in my sixteen years of being alive, and I have to say, Jason's smile was the most genuine. It was the type of smile that asked, "Where the hell have you been hiding?"

I only replied with my name.

"Kennedy." By this time, I thought he would realize my relation to his ex-best friend but his smile never broke. He either never knew about me, or is very obtuse.

"Why have I never seen you before? Usually, I notice everyone," He asked clenching his jaw in question.

"Well, I guess you're not really good at noticing then," I smiled taking another sip of the boiling tomato basil soup my mom made this morning. He continued to scrutinize me, and then I saw him turn his head to the floor. He clenched his jaw more and I felt an uneasiness pass over us.

20

"Is this some joke? Did your mates put you up to this?" He asked harshly. I turned to him calmly and shook my head.

"No. They were a little confused to why I would want to hang out with you, but they didn't stop me. They don't have the right," I responded easily.

"I don't understand...how can someone like you think the same way I do?" I smiled to myself realizing his loneliness. Even if he wants to be different from everyone, he still is a normal boy, with valid feelings, and the occasional doubt. Except, he is a normal boy, with a very different mind.

"Why not?"

Harrison

She asked me to help her with her project.
Me.
Harrison.

It's been three days and I still can't believe it. She said she would come over to the library after school hours on Friday so we could work on her project considering that I love Bukowski *so* much.

My hands have been sweating for 72 hours. My mom was worried that I was coming down with something, but I told her it was nothing. Just a simple case of immense infatuation with a girl who finally talked to me. No big deal.

I couldn't keep my thoughts straight that whole day. Even the thought of her made me lose every common sense I had.

I was seeing her today. Together. Just us. Just hearing my name between her lips was enough. I woke up today in the best mood I've ever been in. Kennedy noticed, but she didn't ask about it. Probably because she knew already. That kid knows everything.

My soccer team yelled at me for not focusing. In fact, every teacher yelled at me to pay attention. I was zoning out far too much. I was thinking of what I would say. What would she ask? How should I respond? Will I fuck up? Will she never talk to me again?

All I want is her to talk to me. I want to hear what her favorite things are and why. I want to see her at her happiest and saddest, just so I can make sure she's real. I want to see her in the best moments of her life. I want to see how she makes her coffee or tea, and how she sits when she reads a book. I want to see her at her worst, so I can try to make it better. I want to see her happy, even if that means in the arms of Kevin, or some other guy that doesn't deserve her sunlight. I'm not saying that I deserve it, because Lord knows that I don't. I just want to be in her warmth, hoping that I could witness the light shining off of her every single day.

I want her to know about me. I want her to care, even if she's pretending. If there is a God, and he sent me the miracle of allowing August to have me, I would spend all my days showing her and the world how we all orbit around her pinky finger. I know she has flaws, like every normal human being, but I love them. Whatever they may be.

Kennedy hates that I love her. I didn't even have to tell her for her to know. She walked into my room one day and started yelling her tiny head off.

"It's not right to put another person's life above your own! You don't even know the real her! You are so fucking in love with this idea of her that you convinced yourself she is the center of, not just your universe, but everyone's! How dare you? Don't you realize what you're doing to yourself? When she's gone, and marries someone else, and forgets who you are, what will you do? Stalk her down, still in love? That's pathetic, fucking pathetic."

"You never been in love Ken, you don't understand. Even if I explain to you, you won't understand!"

"She doesn't even know your fucking name! Wake up, Harrison! Because the next thing you know, she's out there living her own life, with not even the slightest thought of you, and you're stuck in this obsessive idea that she is the sun. She's not the fucking sun, she's a girl who is gorgeous, and uses that to get what she wants. If you can't realize that now, you never will. And you'll die, still thinking of her," With that she stormed out of my room, slamming by door with such force she broke it's hinges and split it halfway.

Kennedy still knows I'm in love with August, but I think she's given up trying to talk (yell) me out of it. I want Kennedy to fall in love one day, and finally understand how it feels. I do wish the best for her, hell she's my little sister, but sometimes I think she either knows too much or not enough. Kennedy never was black or white. All she knows is grey, and all I know is August.

I know that August will have her own life and I'll have mine, but I want her to be a part of mine. I already know where I'm going next fall. I got a scholarship for playing soccer at one of the best schools in the country. I'm happy to go, excited really, but I hope August is in the same school, or at least close by. I feel like my life would be duller without her near.

But if she isn't, I know that I'll have to move on. I will move on, everyone does at some point. But the month of August will always be special to me. I know that everything will remind me of her. Every girl that I will be with will never compare to August. That's what I'm scared about, honestly.

The last bell rung, and I realized I wasted all of English just thinking about her. But with the sound of the last bell, my heartbeat sped up instantly. I only have one more hour until I'm with her. I practically ran over to the library, with only one thought. August.

Emily

I didn't have breakfast today. Not because I didn't want too, but because no one came it in to bring it while I was taking my medicine. I pressed the CALL button about 3,000 times and now my thumb hurts. What a sad Friday.

The door was open except no one was at the desk. I was waiting until someone passed my door, but it's been 45 minutes and no one even made a sound. Suddenly, I heard a far clicking sound meaning that someone opened the door to the treatment section.

FINALLY.

The sturdy footsteps continued to grow louder and closer, which made my stomach growl in victory. The footsteps got close enough that I called out eagerly.

"Is anyone out there?" I just had to make sure it wasn't my vast imagination. The footsteps faltered for a bit, but continued nevertheless. "If anyone is out there, please come to C114, and if you don't want too, at least call someone too. Preferably a nurse! Preferably Sammy!" I yelled. Finally, the footsteps reached my door and a shaggy head popped in.

"Oh, someone is actually in here," he said more to himself than me.

"Did you think it was some ghost or something?" I snarked.

"Yea, kinda." He chuckled and walked inside. He still had his jacket on, and it was wet on his navy blue shoulders. His hair was darkened because it was damp, but you could still see that it was a light brown. He dug his hands into his pockets and looked around the room, probably trying to avoid eye contact with me.

"Did you hear what I said?" He looked at me lost. "A nurse. Can you call a nurse," I rolled my eyes.

"Do you need help?" His blue eyes went frantic, looking at all the wires I was tangled in.

"I just want breakfast," I sighed. He physically relaxed and laughed at his sudden outburst.

"Sorry… I'm just not used to hospitals," he replied sheepishly.

"You're lucky," I said easily. He put his hands in his pocket, and I could tell he wanted to ask about why the hell I was here but that's deemed rude. "Don't worry it's not cancer so you can stop looking at me like I'm about to die any second. I'm just your average teenage girl in the mental ward getting her medicine." I couldn't read his facial expression, but I didn't really want to.

"What type of medicine?" I almost burst out laughing at his question. *Of all things to ask, he asks that one.*

"It's pretty much things that make me less senile and keeps me from lashing out at random people. Some days it works, others… not so much," I explained. He nodded his head, trying to understand but not really comprehending. He looked so awkward, just standing there. He clenched his jaw, and swayed back and forth on his heel. It made me chuckle at his ironic childlike-ness.

"That sucks." That one killed me. I laughed out loud and he looked like I shot him.

"Yea, you're right. It does suck," I smiled after I wiped my tears from laughing too much.

"Did I say something wrong?" He asked slowly.

"No, you didn't. You said exactly what you wanted to, thank you for that," I responded. I put my hand out (the one not tangled in wires), "I'm Emily."

"Sam," he smiled back, and walked over with his hand out as well. His hands were rough, but so were mine. "How long you've been here?" I could almost feel his relaxing curiosity setting in.

"About three months, not that long, but not that short either," I replied.

"Does this place suck as well?" He asked.

"When does a mental institution not suck? I mean, there are worse mental institutions, so I should be lucky I can at least walk around freely here, but it's just so depressing. No one wants to talk, and when people do it's either about what movie we watching on Friday, what's for dinner, and who wants to play cards… completely shitty," I explained, probably more than I should've but sometimes I can't help myself.

"Sounds like hell," he leaned on the wall, captivated by the conversation, "Is it because you're the only teen here, or is it just because you hate old people?" He flashed a grin and I rolled my eyes.

"There are some teens here, but they're all insane. I personally think I'm not that insane, but then again, I'm here for a reason." The machine beeped, signaling the end of my medicine. Sam was on alert, but I grinned at his impulse. I pressed OFF and took all the wires and needles out. I laid them on the bed like I always do, and jumped off fixing my sweatshirt and tightening my sweatpants. Sam was taller than I figured, but still not intimidating. "And I don't hate old people, I'm convinced it is them that hate me," I finished.

I stretched a bit, before walking to the door. "Well, are you going to stay in here or follow me?" He jumped out of his trance and walked behind me as I turned off the room's light and closed the door. My flip flops were making the loudest noise down the empty hallway, while Sam stayed quiet next to me. "So, why are you here?" I asked. It took him some time to answer and he sighed before speaking.

"I was thinking of admitting my mom in here, so I came to check it out," I nodded my head in understatement.

"Well, do you know what ward she will be in?" I asked, wanting to help. He ran a hand through his hair and nodded.

"The bipolar depression ward," He answered in a soft tone. Before opening the door to the main hall, I turned to him.

"Hey, look. I know I shit on this place before, but honestly it's a really good place. It helps people, it really does. And you shouldn't feel bad about putting your mom in here, you are going out of your way to help her. So don't you dare feel ashamed of that, I won't allow you too. And either way, if you're really nervous, I promise to take care of her while she's in here," I rushed, feeling that I stepped into uncomfortable territory.

"You don't even know me, why would you do that for me?" He asked. I punched him in the arm, and rolled my eyes as I opened the door to the main hall.

"We all have to stick together in here, that's just how it works." He smiled widely at me and pushed me back.

"Thank you," he said softly.

"Don't get all chummy with me okay? Now, let me give you a personal tour of this fine establishment," I walked forward, and he followed.

August

I made sure that I arrived early to the library to make it seem that I had to wait on Harrison. He would be spluttering out apologizes before I even knew it and falling directly into my palm. Phase 2 was a go.

Harrison, as I predicted, stumbled into the library pulling his bag behind him. I chuckled at his distorted presence. *What an adorable dork.*

"Am I late? Did I make you wait that long? God, I am so sorry. My teacher was being so annoying and going on and on abo-,"

"You're fine Harrison, breathe," I laughed as I pushed out the seat across from me with my foot for him to sit in. He smiled and placed his bag on the ground beside him as he took a seat. I watched him fumble out three books from Bukowski, along with post-it notes and a notebook. "I feel like I am a bit unprepared," I laughed, waving around my small notebook and my one pencil. He smiled at my gesture and shook his head.

"You'll be fine, I promise." I didn't except his simple words to hit me as hard as they did, but I have to admit it knocked me out for a bit. I had to remember my plan and stick to it.

"Okay, so give me my options Mr. Harrison," I bit my lip and I swear I heard his heart slam into his chest.

"U-um, well I brought all the Bukowski books I have. He has more than these, but I think these are his best." Harrison pushed one of Bukowski's novel that I already read in front of me. "This is called the *Pleasures of the Damned*, it's just a collection of his poems that pretty much kill," He explained it with rich love in his voice, but he was so shy about it. He cleared his voice and took a deep breath.

"My favorite line from this books is, '*the centuries are sprinkled with rare magic/ with divine creatures/ who help us get past the common and extraordinary ills that beset us.*'" I had to stare at him for a minute, letting the words bounce off of his lips into my chest. I bit my lip and smiled.

"That was beautiful Harrison... what's the next one?" I let my voice become a whisper, and I physically saw him shudder. I couldn't help but love the effect I have on this boy, I don't think I'll ever get used to it.

"It's another poetry book of his," He responded.

"I guess you're a sucker for free verse then?" I teased. He rubbed the back of his neck with his right hand, and smiled shyly.

"I'm that easy to read aren't I?" He joked.

"Yes, but very a intriguing read," I played along. He clenched his jaw and pushed forward the second Bukowski book. I could almost see the veins in his arms and hands pulse.

"This one is called *The Last Night of the Earth*. I think one of the best quotes of his are in here," His eyes started to glow as he started to talk about Bukowski again. He was entrancing. '*I tell you such fine music waits in the shadows of hell.*' I know it's short... but I kind of love it," He smiled sheepishly and took deep breath, as if he has been holding it in this whole time.

"I like when you read to me," I stated and I knew it killed him. "What's the last one?"

He cleared his voice before speaking, as if he was in a trance himself. "Um— the next one is called *You Get So Alone at Time That it Just Makes Sense*. It's one of my favorites, once again it's just a collection of poems-," He explained.

"That kills right?" I chuckled as I pushed my hair behind my left ear, "Okay, whats your favorite line from this one?" I asked. I secretly already read this book of Bukowski's. I don't really have a favorite Bukowski because all of them are my favorites. But a part of me just wanted to hear Harrison's voice speak Bukowski's words again. Something about the way he did it was otherworldly.

"Theres so many to choose from...I guess its... '*There is a place in the heart that will never be filled/ a space/ and even during the best moments and the greatest times/ we will know it/ we will know it more than ever/ there is a place in the heart that will never be filled/ and we will wait and wait/ in that space,*'" He licked his lips when he was done, and I had to take a deep breath.

"I really like that one- I think that book is it," I found myself saying. His eyes lit up and his smile stretched across his glowing face.

"Really? I can find another book, if you need another option," he quickly stated.

"I think you convinced me that this one," I pointed to the yellow covered Bukowski bible, "is the one," I smiled.

"I just read you a line..." Harrison mumbled.

"That's all it took," I responded. His eyes immediately softened, and and I felt victorious. I had him- I completely conquered him. The gold in his brown eyes sparked, and they were transfixed on me, as if he was confessing his undying love right then and there. My whole body felt warm with his love embracing me — but on top of that I felt triumphant. Because I had completely conquered him. "Let's get started."

Jason

Kennedy made it her goal to sit with me every lunch from that day. I didn't mind of course, because she agreed with what I said. It felt good to have someone not look at you like a freak. Kennedy did that. She was in the grade below me, but it felt like she was years older than me. Her wisdom took me by surprise, an old soul maybe... I can't put my finger on her. I think that's what I like about her. She's unpredictable.

It was the fifth day in a row that she decided to sit with me. She pulled out her thermos again with another serving of soup and poured one for me as well.

"Another question I have for you," She started (like she usually does), "What were you like when you didn't realize the bullshit?" I sighed and thought about how to answer to question. I heard her waiting patiently for my answer, shaking from the cold. I had to smile at how she always forgets a jacket on days like these; a cold overcast, in contrary to the start of spring in a couple of days. I shrugged off my black jacket, and put it over her before answering her question.

"I was a jock really. Soccer team star with my best friend. We had this whole dream of going to the same college and playing ball. We even made a bet about who will go pro or not," I smiled at the distant memory; nostalgia easing me into its grip. "We used to go to all the parties, and all the girls knew us. We used to get by in class, and the teachers scolded us, but it wasn't like we got in trouble. Life was easy...too easy. And then I realized the bullshit of course...and well- here we are," I ended with a sigh. Remembering what once was is bullshit. There's no changing the past, so there's no use in thinking about it.

32

"What made you stop? I mean— what made you realize the bullshit?" She asked, taking another cautious sip on her soup with one hand, and tightening my jacket around her small body with the other. I followed her in suit by taking a quick sip before answering.

"The bullshit was always there. Bullshit doesn't just appear in thin air. Bullshit has been there since the beginning of humanity, we've just become so oblivious and used to it that it seems part of everyday life. I guess I just noticed it. I just knew there was something always missing, something that didn't add up. I always felt like that, and I finally realized that it was the bullshit I was stuffing myself with. No one tells you about the bullshit, you have to realize it yourself," I babbled. I bit my tongue to stop myself from talking. It was just too easy to speak to her.

"Do you regret it?" She asked softly, as if her question was treading in rough waters. I had to wait a couple of minutes before answering because I was still wondering about it myself. Was it worth losing my best friend? My whole life plan? My outlook on life in general? Was it worth giving up the bullshit? "You don't have to answer that!" She quickly added. "I don't want you to tell me something you aren't sure of. It's such a hard question anyway. I'm sorry for asking," she apologized. I shook my head at her sudden outburst.

"You don't need to be sorry, it was a valid question. I don't really know about the answer to your question, but hell, I don't even know why you care to ask anyway," I confessed. What is this girl's motive? Was I one of her psychology projects? Was she just curious, or did she really care?

"I asked because I've noticed the bullshit too. I think I always have. I'm just better at hiding it, unlike you,

Bullshit Boy," she smiled into her soup. I chuckled and rolled my eyes at the sound of my infamous nickname.

"When did you realize then?" I asked, in complete awe of this girl sitting beside me. She bit her lip and cocked her head to the side, like she was really thinking about this one.

"I guess it was in middle school. I was walking down the hallway one afternoon, and overheard every conversation that germinated at each locker and each corner. And it kind of just hit me. It didn't feel like an epiphany…in fact it felt depressing as fuck. I realized that none of that matters. That everyone in that hallway then, and everyone in the hallways now, are temporary. There's not even a guarantee we'll all be here tomorrow. And they are all there, talking about everyone else's business and other things that don't matter as if they are there for eternity. I think that was when I realized the bullshit all around us," She answered easily.

"Do you regret it?" I asked, mimicking her. She turned to me and laughed with her hearty brown eyes. She took the final sip of her soup and stared at the Bullshit Eaters across from us as if she was taking them in, pore by pore.

"No, I don't. It's not the majority opinion at all, but I rather know the truth and be this pessimistic, then drowning in ignorance my whole life. I think the knowledge is worth it," she sighed out, hugging my jacket closer to her goose bump filled body.

"I believe you make an excellent point," I responded truthfully.

"I know," she smirked.

34

Kennedy

I had to watch Harrison drive us home with the stupidest grin on his face, and I knew it all had to do with a certain girl named after a month. I didn't even want to ask about it. I didn't even want to talk about her again. She was going to be the death of him, and I already did all I can do to help him get out of the caves of hell. Yet, he seems to really like it there.

I crossed my arms over my chest and looked out the window, trying to escape from my brother's oozing fabricated happiness.

"Someone looks pissed," he broke the silence when a commercial came on the radio station we were listening to.

"Someone is pissed," I responded quickly. I didn't even have to look at him to know that he rolled his eyes.

"Haven't you already said enough about her?" Harrison asked, and I knew he was referring to August.

"Obviously not," I mumbled in my state of annoyance. I heard him take a deep breath, and I mentally prepared myself for the rant about love and August he always gives to me.

"Mom is out for the night, and Dad is staying over in the city for work, so we're gonna have to order in," Harrison stated, taking me by surprise at the sudden change of topic. "She said not to have anyone over, and no parties," Now it was my turn to roll my eyes.

"Why are you telling me this, its not like I ever invite people over anyway," I retorted.

"If you did I won't tell," Harrison said.

"But I don't want anyone over."

"I'm just saying if you did I wouldn't tell."

"What are you trying to get at here?" I sat up a bit straighter.

"It's just… you never…none of your friends come over," Harrison cleared his throat.

"I don't have friends, I have very good aquatints,"

"That's my point," I sighed. "You're already a junior Ken, and you never had anyone over. I don't even know if you have friends at all. Doesn't that sound a bit abnormal?"

"Sorry I'm not at popular as you."

"Come on Ken, you know I don't mean it that. You're this great, intelligent, funny and annoying as hell girl, I don't know why you don't have anyone to hang out with," Harrison's snuck a glance at me, probably to see if I was even more pissed at him or not.

"I don't like getting involved with people. It's not like anyone I meet here I will keep for the rest of my life. You should know that more than anyone right now," I eased into. His expression turned solemn and I knew I tripped on a triggered wire.

"I didn't leave Jason, Kennedy. He left me," Harrison responded sharply. I kept my mouth shut for the rest of the car ride. I usually wasn't so snappy, but something about August made me feel completely agitated. Like an itch I couldn't scratch. Or a piece of lint I couldn't get off of my sweater. Or a girl seducing everyone to play out of her soft, manicured hands.

I didn't tell Harrison I was hanging around Jason. I knew he would freak out, but I also knew that Jason would freak out if he found out that I was Harrison's sister. At first, I wanted to do this to persuade Jason back into Harrison's life, and smack some reality back into his entranced face. But now learning about Jason, and why he did what he did, I don't really know how to feel. The Bullshit Boy wasn't as bad as everyone said he was. I couldn't help the clench of my stomach when he put his jacket over me (because I foolishly forgot mine) with ease. As if he did that to every person- male and female.

He is pessimistic, granted, but there's something optimistic about his pessimism. He speaks of the bullshit eaters, but being aware of it is the first step for improvement. I think he is secretly trying to become a better person. Why else would he completely remove himself from everyone he's ever known to sit glumly on a curbside? If he does that at school, I wonder what he does everywhere else.

I knew I shouldn't be thinking this much about Jason Smith — the town's own infamous fuck up. He had everything. Money, popularity, beautiful looks, luck, talent… I could go on but that would only make me feel worse. Then, out of nowhere, he just stopped. Stopped playing soccer, denied his scholarship, dropped out of all his pervious classes, distanced himself from everyone he once knew. And that was that. People tried to talk to him, of course, but he gave the same response he would give everyone else that asked. *"I don't talk to bullshitters."*

After a while, people just didn't want to put up with his crap anymore, and he settled into the shadows of the curbside and corner desks in the back of classrooms.

Everyone gave up on him — but I wasn't going to let him go that easily. I knew who he was before, I knew how he made everyone feel. What he needs right now is someone that won't give up on him. He's just one of those people.

"Are you gonna get out of the car or sleep in there for the night?" Harrison spoke up as he closed the door on the drivers side. I watched him walk up our driveway and enter the house without turning back.

And then I had an idea.

Harrison

I didn't mean to be so hard on Kennedy, but she seems to always get under your skin. I want to say that she is like every younger sister, but I would be lying. She probably knows more than me, or even my parents. She has always been so intelligent, and she always seems to be a step further than most people. Secretly, I've always been a little bit jealous — but that doesn't mean I listen to what she says about August.

That afternoon in the library made me fall for her more than I ever have. It just showed me that I could never get over her. Even in the next life, I'd probably still love her. She reminds me of Kennedy; with that look that she's always a step further. It should terrify me (and it does) but I can't turn away. My hands are still shaking since after I helped her pick what book to read, and she easily took my phone from my hand and added her contact. She didn't even make eye contact with me as she punched my own number in her phone and said that she will call if she's dying with questions. She made it a joke, and I know I should've laughed, or showed some sign that I was alive, but I physically couldn't. She thanked me in her siren voice and walked out the door, as if she was never there.

I had to sit down for an extra fifteen minutes to steady my breathing. She's making it harder and harder to go on. I pushed her to the back of my mind and picked up the house phone to order dinner.

"Utopia Pizza, how may I help you?" A high pitched voice entered my ear.

"Hey, can I order for delivery one large pizza and-," I held the phone to my chest before calling out for Kennedy, "Ken! What do you want from Utopia Pizza?" I awaited her response, but nothing came. I called out her name again, and groaned at the silence that answered me back. She was probably upstairs with her headphones on. "I'll call you back, sorry," I said to the girl on the phone and hung up. I ran up to Kennedy's room and knocked on the door. "Ken, come on, I'm just asking for your order and I'll bug off," Silence greeted me again. Out of frustration, I opened Kennedy's door to find a cold wind from her empty room.

My mind wandered and my skin pricked out of uneasiness. I ran back downstairs and looked in all the places she might have been. Except, she was nowhere. I ran a hand through my hair, now fucking freaking out. The last place I saw her was the car — did she actually stay in there? I ran to the front door, and swung it open to see an empty driveway.

Holy fuck.

Emily

I sat down in the old, blue couch across from the activity room watching everyone make a fool of themselves. I probably looked fucking weird too, with my oversized grey hoodie covering my head, and my dark leggings tucked into my black boots filled with scrape marks. I probably was shooting daggers at everyone.

It was interpretive dance night. Some local hippie always came in and moved everyone who wanted to participate into the activity room to dance. She would put on some weird bird noises, or whale noises, and yell at everyone to feel the music, or be the music. In other words, I rather throw up. It sucked as well, that everyone loved Interpretive Dance nights. Even some of the teens decided to show up. It was pitiful. Tonight was, you guessed it, whale noises from the Atlantic. Seriously, I wanted to burn my eyes, but I couldn't tear them away.

My head snapped to the sudden touch on my shoulder to see the desk nurse, Tessa, with her hand resting upon it. "Instead of glaring at them, you could join them Emily," she smiled. I gave her a scrunched up face and shook my head.

"Absolutely not — I would be caught dead before doing…that," I cringed watching the scene before me.

"Well, I was thinking you should do something active after your three day suspension lifted," Tessa responded. Tessa was a nice lady, she was in her late 30's, and she actually works here because she chose to. I know, weird. Nevertheless, she always comes in here with her optimistic attitude, happy face, and big ass wedding ring. I have this awesome curse of finding things to hate.

"Well, *I* was thinking that you should go back into your cubicle and leave me alone," I replied without making eye contact, but I felt her hand retract at my words, "Or better yet — go join the loons. I bet you would have a ball," I smiled eerily at her, causing her to shuffle away. I hugged my sweatshirt tighter around my body and continued glaring at the whale imposters.

The main door dinged open behind me, and all the whale imposters and I snapped our heads to the sound. It was 7 PM which isn't visiting hours, so of course we all would be curious whom from the outside world was coming inside this looney bin. Me, being the closest, was the first one to see who the screams were coming from.

I watched as two security guards, and two other nurses restricted a middle-aged woman pulling away from their grasps. Her face was red, probably from the anger and tears, and her eyes were panicked from being in a new, scary place. Her clothes were even disoriented. Her dirty-blond hair was all over the place, as well as her green blouse. Her black slacks swung around every time she tried to kick herself free. Thank god her nails were cut, or she could've done some serious damage to Steve (one of the security guards). Tessa, ran from her desk to get the tranquilizer shot, which we all felt once or twice. She injected the hurtful needle into the woman's thigh, and almost immediately calmed down. The two nurses and security guards guided her down the hallway to the containment unit, which she will spend the night until she calmed down and understand what's happening to her. Then she will be let outside and moved to her required unit, until she's better.

The steps were simple, because all of us already have been through them (well at least most of them).

42

While everyone was watching the woman being carried down to the containment unit, my eyes found their ways to familiar blue ones. Except they weren't as shiny as they were before; they were filled to the brim with red, hot tears. Seeing those eyes made my chest collapse twenty times over.

Without even realizing it, I ran over to Sam and pulled him into a hug. Not a shitty one, but the ones my mother used to give me. The ones where the person's head is hiding in the crook of your neck, while your arms bind to them, holding them with every fiber of your being hoping you can take their pain away. I could feel his tears fall onto my sweatshirt and onto my collarbone, but I disregarded them completely. All I can do is hold him like this — the same way I wished someone would've held me now. I kept on mumbling *it's okay* into his red ears, hoping for the love of god that he understands, and that it will only get better from here. Because it will, because it has to.

August

I sat on my white bed staring at my phone with fidgety hands. *Why the hell was I so nervous?* My black phone stared mockingly back at me, probably confused with my hesitation. Calling guys is the easiest thing to do, I've done it thousands of times, but for some reason I can't find the power within myself to call Harrison. As if on cue, my phone started vibrating, causing me to flinch. I quickly picked it up and awaited the caller to say something.

"Babe, are you home right now?" I couldn't help but feel disappointed hearing Kevins voice. I ran a hand though my hair and sighed inwardly.

"Yea, I had to do some homework," I replied.

"Okay, I was wondering where you headed off to. You usually wait by my car, but when you weren't there I was worried," I smiled quietly, appreciating his concern.

"No need, I just had a lot to do and I didn't want to fall behind," I responded playing with the rings on my fingers.

"Well, you up for Mike's party? We can just sit and watch a movie if you'd like, I noticed you've been distracted lately," I clenched my jaw at Mike's sweetness. Everyone was so sweet to me. It felt like I had this cavity for seventeen years.

"Um...," I bit my lip, thinking of what to do. I was too anxious and tired to party. But I also didn't want to hang out with Kevin either. "My dad is coming home today, so I'm going to wait for him," I responded without missing a beat.

"Really? Why didn't you tell me? How long was it this time? What... seven months?" He sounded interested, but thats what they always sound like. I always have this pang of guilt for not loving Kevin as much as he loves me. When

44

he first said he loved me a year ago, I easily lied back. But, he was such a sweet guy. Sometimes I would even say something I knew was controversial or rude, just so I can get a rile out of him. But he would just keep his cool, and side with me. Honestly, I just wanted someone to yell at me.

"Eight months actually, and I'm sorry for not telling you. It was kind of sudden for me too," I didn't lie to him — my dad was coming, but I didn't tell him that I probably won't be here when he does.

"That's alright babe...I just want you to tell me these things. I'll miss you at Mike's party, I hope you have a good time with your dad. We still on for the weekend though?" I shut my eyes feeling a headache coming on. On the weekend was another party, a girl named Hannah this time.

"Yea, of course," I said in my most happiest tune.

"Great," I could practically hear him smile, "I love you, see you tomorrow,"

"Love you too, bye," I hung up the phone letting the words slip out as easily as it was the first time. I liked Kevin. Lacrosse team, good grades, great family, not bad looking, and loved me of course. But parties was all we had in common. Sure, we go on some dates, but it's usually me asking him questions and playing along with his lame jokes. I thought that maybe if I was with someone everyone would stop treating me so delicately, but it was just the same as it always has been. Boring, and predictable.

With my phone still in my hand, I used the last shred of courage to call up the name I've been staring at.

The phone picked up after two rings, and I smirked at Harrison's desperateness.

"Hey, its August," I stated with more confidence I actually possessed.

"Um… hey, hi," I first thought his stuttering was because I called, but something felt too rushed.

"Is everything okay?" I asked, actually curious. I heard him groan on the other line, and take a deep breath.

"My sister is missing."

Jason

My mom was yelling on the phone when I heard a knock at the front door. She only stopped yelling to give me the *get-the-damn-door* look. I rolled my eyes from the couch I was lying on, and slugged over to the front door. I opened it, stepped outside and immediately shut the door when I saw who it was.

"What are you doing here?" I asked quickly, hoping Kennedy wouldn't hear my mothers distant shouting.

"A hello would be nice too," She smiled as she placed her hands into her brown jacket. I shook my head at her coincidental bad timing.

"Hello Kennedy, now why are you here?" I asked again with a hint of a smile.

"Picking you up, lets go," She started walking away, but I grabbed her arm before she could fully turn around.

"Wait, you can't just show up at my house and tell me we're going somewhere. Aren't you only sixteen anyway?" I asked calmly.

"I think the question you're looking for is *Oh Kennedy, where are we going?*" She brushed off her shoulder.

"I can't go anywhere right now…" I trailed off, as my mothers loud shouts echoed behind me. Silence settled and I saw Kennedy looking from me to the door. She could probably hear my mother, she wasn't even trying to be quiet about it. I saw hazel eyes calculate what was happening, and they slowly found mine again.

"Is something bad happening right now?" Her question was so innocent I just had to laugh a little.

"Kind of, but if you came here on any other evening I would've gone with you. Hell, I would've even started the car," I joked, retracting my grip from her arm.

47

"Is there anything I can do to help?" She asked.

"I'm sorry, but this is kind of serious," I felt so bad turning her down. She drove all the way here to hang out with me, and I wasn't lying when I told her that I would've gone.

"That's okay, I understand. I hope everything works out, I'm sorry I intruded without calling beforehand," She looked down at her feet. I shook my head immediately, hoping she doesn't truly think that.

"Are you kidding? Don't ever apologize, just a lot of shit is happ-," My front door suddenly swung open, and my mother stood in the doorframe about to yell at me, until she saw Kennedy.

"Oh...," Her eyes were wide as she looked from me to Kennedy. I clenched my jaw, hating my luck right now. The last thing I needed was my mom to embarrass me in front of Kennedy. The last thing I needed was Kennedy thinking I'm some cliche fucked up teen. "Oh...," My mom repeated again. She tried to compose herself the best way she could, and put on a fake smile. "Hello, I'm Jason's mom. I don't think we've met," She extended her hand out to Kennedy and I thought I was dying.

"Hello, I'm Kennedy. Jason and I are friends at school," She shook my mothers hand with a bright smile.

"If I may ask, what brings you here?" She asked, but I don't think Kennedy noticed that it was strained. I wanted to step in, but my mouth restricted me.

"Well... I know it's late, but I just wanted to hang out with Jason for a while. I'm sorry if I came at a bad time... and out of the blue..." Kenned trailed off, and I quickly gained consciousness and grabbed her hand, leading her to her car in by the curb.

"I'll see her off!" I yelled back to my mom, who was definitely going to interrogate her more if I didn't pull Kennedy away fast enough. I let go of her hand when Kennedy climbed into her car. I closed the door and leaned into the open window. "You have no idea how embarrassed and sorry I am," I started shaking my head not believing what just happened.

"It's okay," Kennedy chuckled, "I know a lot of people who still get permission from their mom to hang out," she immediately laughed and I followed suit.

"Oh god, please do not make fun of me for this," I replied.

"It'll be our secret," She smirked at me and started the car.

"Aren't you a little bit too young to be driving by yourself?" I shouted as she pulled away slowly.

"Aren't you a little bit too old to be asking your mom for permission?" She laughed back at me and drove off.

She's never going to let me live that down.

But a part of me doesn't want her to.

Kennedy

Not only was that one of the weirdest, terrifying, and funniest things that ever happened to me — but Harrison is going to kill me. Not give me a lecture on how to never steal his car again and disappear, but actually lock me in my room and starve me to death. I bet he is freaking out right now, and it would all have been avoided if I didn't forget my phone at school.

I hope he didn't call the police, because then I would actually be damned to hell by my parents as well. All I wanted was to hang out with Jason, we both needed it today. Just to get away for a while, and the way his mom was yelling before, something told me he really wanted to leave.

A dark thought entered my mind as I pulled onto my street. *What if I was turning to Harrison?* I tried to shake the thought, but of course, my mind never listens. I didn't love Jason, that would be insane. But I did care about the guy, and I wanted to just be with him for a couple of hours… was that so bad? He was my friend— one of the only ones I care about.

Unlike what Harrison thought, I did have friends at school. I had a whole group, mostly from the photography club. Out of all of them Hannah was my closest friend, but that doesn't mean I can take her bullshit every single day. Jason doesn't do bullshit, and thats what I admire about him. When we talk, we actually speak about things that matter. We don't talk about anyone else's business. We have debates sometimes from what we learned in class, or what was floating in our minds that day. When I want to hear something more than who was wearing what, and who hooked up with who, I sit with Jason and ask him what he thinks of different universes, and who would he be in a different version of life. If I was caught asking those kinds of questions to my friend group, they would laugh and pretend I was just making a joke. Just your common everyday bullshitters.

Jason, on the other hand, looks at me like I know what I'm talking about. And the way his mind thinks is amazingly sad, but inspiring at the same time. Why wouldn't I want to hang out with him?

Yet, if Harrison found out, I'd be killed again. Repeatedly. I just wanted to figure out what happened. Simple question, except such a difficult answer. Just what happened to everyone? What happened to the Harrison who kept his love hidden until now? What happened to the Harrison that would come home happy with his best friend talking about college? What happened to my brother who had his life together, who had everything together? Now he's practically tripping over his love for some promiscuous girl that knows too much, not even talking about college, not even talking to his best friend.

Then there's Jason, who has gone off the track completely. Who is now considered as Bullshit Boy. Who had everything put together, and now can't seem to find his way back. It's not that I feel bad for him, it's what happened to him that bugs me. What happened that made him become Bullshit Boy? Why did Harrison just let him go? Why did Jason leave in the first place? Why does everyone leave at some point?

Why must people continue to be temporary?

I always hated thinking things like this, it made me so sad. It made me sad to think that Harrison would go to his dream college, play soccer, and still be in love with some girl that doesn't deserve him. It makes me sad to think that

Jason still doesn't know where to go. It makes me sad to think that everyone I know right now is so confused and lost that they don't even realize they're even lost yet. It makes me sad that I'm the only person that realizes this.

I don't want to act like I have my life together, because I'm just a sixteen year old girl in junior year still figuring shit out. But it's depressing to think that even a year from now I still won't have my act together— maybe even longer than that. And that is what terrifies me.

I had to laugh at myself at how cliche I was being. All I need to be doing now is getting home in one piece, only to be torn apart by my loving (and probably going insane) older brother.

Harrison

"Do you have any idea where she could've gone? A friend's house? The park? A store? The movies perhaps? Maybe she just went for a drive?" August was trying to write all the places down where Kennedy could've gone while I paced around my living room.

"I don't know, honestly, it's so horrible to say but I don't know what friends she has at school. Usually, she just comes home and does her homework. If she wants to go out, it's usually by herself. She's just one of those girls, but she never leaves without telling me. And its usually walking distance, because she never would do this. She never would take my car and just drive away. For fucks sake! She's just sixteen!" I ran my hand through my hair, exasperated and nervous at the same time. My heartbeat was most likely going off the charts: my sister was missing, and the girl who I have been in love with for my whole life is sitting in my living room helping me.

If this isn't wonderfully fucked up, I don't know what is.

"Does she usually do a lot of things on impulse? She doesn't seem like the type…" August said, trying to think of other places. But all I could focus on was my blood boiling. I can't decide if this is my worst nightmare, or favorite dream.

"No…never. Not that I know of… Kennedy is so fucking confusing sometimes, but she's never done anything like this. Not this dangerous," I mentioned pacing faster. In a quick moment, August is right in front of me with her hands only shoulder, stopping me in my tracks.

"Harrison, calm down. She's fine, I promise. The only person who won't be fine is you if you keep pacing like that. Now, sit and breathe. We are going to find her," Her hands were burning through my shirt, but I obeyed each word. I sat down on the couch, trying to steady my breathing. She sighed and sat down next to me, pushing me the notebook on the brown table in front of us. "Now write down places she would go, we will hit those places first. And then from there on, we will ask people if they've seen her and where she usually goes and who she hangs out with. With those people and information, I have no doubt that we will find her. You just have to trust me okay?" She explained. I smirked at her thoroughness and took the pen and paper in my hand.

"You are eerily good at this... do you lose things a lot or something?" I tried to joke to make my breathing ease. She smiled back at me and shrugged.

"Something like that," She responded and tapped the paper. I started to write down every place I could remotely think Kennedy would go, and handed the paper back to August. "Good, now lets get into my car and start searching. We can probably get in five places before sundown, but after that it'll be a little bit harder. No worries though, we can do this," August shrugged her coat on and waited for me to follow suit. I just had to shake my head a little and pinch myself to make sure this was really happening.

I was worried out of my mind about Kennedy, but with August in my house willing to help me, I honestly thought this was a dream. I never seen this side of her too. She was demanding and intelligently thinking, while I sit there gaping at her like some old rotten potato. She was blinding me I swear.

She was heading to my front door when I finally caught up with her. I opened the door and August walked out in front of me, while I followed right behind. My eyes immediately darted towards my grey truck as Kennedy slid out.

I felt the biggest weight lift off my chest as I ran towards her and pulled her into my arms.

"Jesus Christ Ken, did you want me to die from a heart attack. I was so fucking worried. Don't you ever do that again!" I shouted pulling her back to see her face. Her eyes were wide and her mouth was trying to form words, but she looked like she was in shock. "And don't fucking take my car!" I added angrily.

"I-I'm sorry...I just wasn't..."

"Thinking? Yea, you weren't. I was going insane, Ken. Just tell me when you're going out, I'll drive you anywhere...just Jesus....don't do that again," I let her go and gave a big sigh. Her eyes suddenly started glaring behind me, which made me more nervous than I've ever been. I cleared my throat and backed away to make room for August. She smiled and gave an exasperated breath.

"We were just about to uproot the whole town to look for you," She laughed harmoniously, "Thank you for saving us the embarrassment. I'm glad you're okay, your brother over here was having a mini panic attack,".

"I don't know why you care," Kennedy snapped, and I immediately glared at her.

"I'm sorry, she doesn't mean that," I said through clenched teeth. I turned to August and pushed Kennedy towards the door, hoping she would go fucking inside this time. I watched her this trudge into the house, leaving the door open a little bit for me. I ran a hand through my hair and looked back to August, smiling sheepishly at me. "She's...difficult. I'm so sorry you had to come all the way here for no reason," I apologized, rubbing the back of my neck. She shook her head, her smile never faltering.

"Please Harrison, it's the least I can do for helping me. We're friends, when my friend is missing a sister, a good friend would most likely help them find her," She chuckled and I swear my heart stopped.

"But you probably had better things to do tonight then help me find my sister who turned out to be right where I left her."

"I was just going to stay home. But even if I was busy, I still would've dropped everything to help you," She responded while backing up to her car. Everything that she said to me gives me goosebumps and I hope it had become too dark for her to see them.

"Thank you, August...really, it means a lot," I willed my words not to sound too desperate. She smiled at me and laughed.

"Of course," She opened the door to her car and slid in, while I closed the door behind her.

"Oh," I stared as I just remembered, "Why did you call me in the first place? I'm just curious, because if you didn't then you wouldn't have come here," I babbled. She pulled on her seatbelt, and pushed her hair out of her face.

"I had a question about the book you gave me to borrow, but it's all good now. I'll ask you again after school on... Monday right?" She asked, cocking her head to the right.

"Yea, Monday," I responded, not hiding the wide smile engraved into my face.

"Great, I'm looking forward to it," She smiled back, as she pulled out of my driveway. "Oh, and next time you think your sister is missing, just call me," She joked before she sped off down my street.

I'm ridiculously in love with this girl and it's just going to get worse from here on out.

Emily

"Just do it. Fucking do it, I dare you," I threatened through my teeth. Woodstock smiled at me cockily, and pushed his queen directly across from my king.

"Checkmate," He wheezed. I banged the table, and cursed under my breath.

"This is insane, you're definitely cheating," I hissed, crossing my arms over my chest. Woodstock leaned back and grinned with the couple of teeth he still had.

"I told you I couldn't be defeated little girl," Woodstock shrugged.

"You're full of shit Woods, how can someone win five times in a row?" I asked exasperated.

"I've been in here longer than you," He coughed.

"You've been alive longer than anyone, let's just face it. You're practically an artifact," I smiled as he gave a hearty laugh. He was about to respond, but he nodded towards the entrance door. I turned around to see Sam standing on the side, waiting for me to be done. He still looked distraught, but of course he would be. He had to see his mom like that — no one should see their mom the way Sam saw his. I saluted a goodbye to Woodstock and his infamous checkerboard table as I walked toward Sam.

"You know, usually when people leave mental institutions, they don't particularly keep coming back," I smiled at him putting my hands in my pockets. He chuckled and shook his head at my lame joke. "How are you?" I asked sincerely.

"Better than I was. But it's still hard to talk about and come to terms with," He honestly replied.

"Trust me, it took me a long time to come to terms with being in here. But once you do, it really becomes easier. It

58

will get easier, and this is the best place she could be at this point," I reassured, "and I'm also here, so you have nothing to worry about." He gave me a soft smile and sighed while looking down the hall his mom was carried down.

"Is she still in there?" He asked carefully. I looked down the same hallway, and bit my lip.

"The usual time in there is two days, so she most likely will come out by today. Only if she's calmed down though. But it honestly isn't as bad as it seems, Sam. I mean— I've been in there more times than I can count. She's really in good hands," I carefully thought about what I was going to say next. "Um… I hope you don't um…beat yourself up about putting her in here. You shouldn't ever have that weight on your shoulder."

He nodded slowly at me, while still gazing down the hallway where his mom is resting. My heart felt heavy for him, he didn't deserve to feel this way when he was so extraordinary.

"So… why were you threatening that old man? I thought old people hated you, not the other way around?" He asked, immediately glowing again. I laughed, recalling our first encounter.

"That's Woodstock, he is the only exception," I replied, still grinning. One of Sam's eyebrows raised curiously as he crossed his arms.

"Woodstock? Like the little yellow bird from *Charlie Brown*?" He asked. I nodded quickly, chuckling at his completely confused expression. "Now I have to ask why."

"That man over there, is one of the most bitter, and oldest fellows I have ever met in my entire life. He has been through two world wars, and fought in each on. Didn't even bother going to Vietnam just because he didn't want to. He won the purple heart more times than the amount of

59

teeth he has left, and I'm convinced he can secretly read minds," I explained while watching Sam stare shockingly at Woodstock. "Because he's short as hell, has a moderately high pitched voice, and was known to move quickly in the army, people used to call him Woodstock. And he also actually went to Woodstock, and practically ran the whole thing," I sighed while Sam's mouth dropped.

"Holy shit, that guy is amazing," Sam responded.

"I know, he's a fucking legend, and nobody knows," I replied, feeling sorry for old Woodstock. He was persuading Mary Jane to play checkers again. Yet, last time that happened he asked for her number in the middle of the game and she almost broke his fingers.

"When are you getting out of here?" Sam suddenly asked. I bit my lip again and thought about the date I've memorized.

"Actually next month, on the eighteenth. I was supposed to get out the last Friday of this month, but I was put on suspension which made my day move to a later date," I explained, trying very hard not to show my eagerness. I have been looking forward to this date for the last eight months. I could finally get out of this place, and feel like a normal person once again. Except, my annoying self-conscious had to start acting up. A part of me was deathly afraid of going back into the world, because it was the world that made me come here in the first place. I didn't know whether I was ready or not to come out.

Nevertheless, I felt better. I felt way better than I did. I've been getting therapy, and been learning how to say what I want to say. Granted, I say too much now, but it was better than before. I just didn't want to end up back here. I just didn't want to end up back to where I was.

"Are you better?" Sam's innocent question matched his pure eyes and I had to chuckle at his expression.

"I sure do hope so," I replied with a sigh. He nodded with a smile and I saw his cheeks turn a shade of pink.

"So, maybe on the nineteenth next month we can hang out...or something. Only if you want to, of course," Sam cleared his throat. I could feel my cheeks burn and I laughed awkwardly.

"You are aware that you're... asking out a mental girl?" I slowly recited.

"Yes," He laughed, "I'm aware."

"Okay, I just wanted to clarify," I played with my fingers like a middle schooler.

"So, the nineteenth?"

"The nineteenth," and suddenly, I had another day to look forward to.

August

"Oh, and next time you think your sister is missing, just call me." I flashed him a bright smile, and drove away down his street. In my mind I knew that I conquered him already, and I'm just waiting for a chance to destroy. Yet, somewhere in my chest I was relieved his sister was okay, and I was thankful that my hands started to shake after I left Harrison's house. I gripped my steering wheel tighter, and started to count in my head; ridding myself of any thoughts to come. The numbers silenced my memories and I relaxed a bit when my phone started to ring. I hoped it was a drunk Kevin, asking me— scratch that— slurring me to pick him up and drive him home. It was a perfect distraction for me. Yet, a familiar number was on my screen and I clenched my jaw in reluctance. This wasn't the distraction I wanted. I picked up the phone and put it on speaker to hear a roar of a voice come through.

"Where are you?" It was a simple question, but I could feel all the heat from my skin radiate from my body.

"Driving home," I replied coldly.

"Where were you?" He asked, sternly.

"At a friend's house. What does it matter now, I'm on my way home. In fact, I'm pulling into the driveway right now," I snapped. I heard a click on the other end and shut off the engine with a groan. I rather be anywhere, literally anywhere right now. After stepping out of my car and locking it, I walked to the front door to await the grinch of a man I call my father.

"How was Hong Kong?" I asked, trying to make conversation as I put my coat away.

"What friend was this?" I sighed inaudibly.

"You don't know him," I replied.

"Him?" I heard his voice clip as I shut the closet door.

"Yes, father. Him. As in male. I have a male friend, shocking, I know." Sarcasm laced my words, and I knew I would see his angry face as soon as I stepped into the kitchen.

He was sitting at the table, still with his grey suit on, looking robotic as ever. Papers were in front of him, and his three phones were all faced down. A glass of red wine was on his far right, and half way done. His jaw was locked as well — thanks to my sarcastic remark.

"So, you're not going to answer my question?" No response. "I'm guessing Hong Kong was shit then." I concluded as I grabbed a bottle of water from the fridge. I heard him rustle some papers, and his phone (at least one of them), buzzed a couple of times. I heard him say his name and listen for a couple of minutes. I then watched him slowly pick up all his papers and the two other phones and place them in a black bag neatly.

"Alright. Is that all? Yes…See you at 10 AM." And with that the phone call ended.

"Where?" I asked numbly.

"Canada." He replied with the same tone, maybe even colder.

"At least we'll still be in the same continent this time," I said, trying to warm-up the icicles in the room. He didn't answer, just packed up his things, and put his glass of whine in the sink. "When will you be back?" I managed to ask.

"In 9 weeks," he replied, and headed upstairs.

I watched him retreat to his bedroom, most likely getting more clean clothes and then searching for some sleep before he left in the morning. I wanted to yell at him, I wanted him to yell at me. I wanted just some sort of fucking conversation without him looking at me with his granite stare. I knew it wasn't worth thinking about, so I finished my water, threw it away, and followed his footsteps upstairs. His door was locked, not like it mattered, and I made my way over to mine, not even letting myself look down the hall to the other room I haven't opened in years. The air seemed easier in my room, and I was too tired to do anything. I laid on my bed and looked out my window, watching the night breathe. I wonder if he loved the night as much as I do.

"August!" I flinched at my name suddenly, and quickly ran over to my window. I have to admit that my heart dropped a little when I realized that it was Kevin. I don't know why.

"What the fuck Kev?" I scolded, wondering if he really was that drunk.

"I missed you, so I came to see you," he slurred, and I groaned.

"You can't be here! Did you drive?" I asked, hoping he didn't do anything stupid.

"I walked of course... I wouldn't do anything to make you worry." He smiled dumbly. I ran my hand down my face, sleepiness drifting from me.

"I'll bring you home, give me a second," I called out. Odds are my dad is in the shower and getting ready for bed, so I had time to sneak out. I'll either wait at Kevins house, or sleep in my car somewhere until he leaves. He never says goodbye anyway, so he won't even notice that I left before him. Hopefully, he won't notice my car gone. But if he does, I couldn't care less.

I walked downstairs, my keys in hand. The late air bit at my cheeks, but a part of me liked it. I walked around to my side of the house, and saw Kevin lying on the ground

64

mumbling my name over and over again. I hated him. When he was sober he was better, of course, but I hated him. I hate that he latches himself onto me, I hate that he thinks we will stay together for college, I hate that he thinks I love him, and I hate that he thinks he loves me. He doesn't know anything about me, no one does.

I grabbed him up by his arm, and threw it over my shoulders to make it easier for him to walk.

"Oh August, are you mad at me?" His alcohol breath stung my eyes.

"I'm fucking furious." I replied through clenched teeth. I got to my car, and helped him into the passenger side. I put his seatbelt on, and also grabbed a bag from the back just in case he wanted to empty his stomach.

I started the car and pulled out before my dad could hear it. I drove with the radio on a low hum, and Kevin humming along to it, while playing with the bag I gave him.

"I'm sorry August, I love you," He said pouting. I glanced at him angrily, and looked back to the road. "I know I fucked up okay...just don't hate me." He whined, "I wouldn't live with myself if you hated me. I wouldn't know how to go on."

"Yes, you would," I snapped. "You would go on just like you went on before I knew you."

"What are you saying?" Kevin asked, suddenly sounding sober.

"I'm saying grow up Kev. I won't always be here to drive you home after you party too hard, or when you need somebody to say I love you back." I didn't mean to sound so harsh to him, but I think I was on edge all today. I knew my dad was coming back and that already put me in a horrible mood, and when I called Harrison and he said that his sister was missing all of my unwanted memories came back to me. Now, Kevin is probably wondering if I'm breaking up with him and I should care. I should put my August charm on, and pretend that he's the best thing that ever happened to me. I should tell him I love him, and promise to never part even if college takes us away. I should lie — I always do anyway.

But today...for some reason today, I wasn't his August. I wasn't the August everyone loved and adored. I was me.

"Is that what you think of me?" Kevin asked.

"With you pissed drunk, and me driving you home at midnight, because you walked all the way to my house just to say I miss you... yea, thats what I think of you Kev," I clenched my teeth.

"Fine, next time I won't come to you," he snapped back.

"Next time don't fucking drink too much," I retorted.

"You're not my mother."

"Are you fucking kidding me, Kevin? Of course I'm not your goddamn mother, but I don't want to wake up the next morning finding out that you got killed in a drunk driving accident you fucking dumbass!" I started shouting, not knowing I was gripping my steering wheel with my nails.

"I wouldn't do something that stupid!" He shouted back.

"I don't know that, hell, you don't know that!" I replied.

"I came to you, didn't I?"

"That's not the point," I exasperated.

"Right, the point is not being as dumb as your brother, got it."

I screeched the car to a stop, and opened the door to his side. "Get out." I demanded. He looked at me like I was crazy.

"August, I didn't mean-,"

"Get. Out. Now." I demanded coldly. He stared at me for a few minutes, probably shit scared and shocked to see me like this. All he ever knew was the kind, sweet, angel everyone was familiar with. Not this. Not me.

With stumbling steps, he slid out from the car and I didn't hesitate to speed off. I dropped him off at the beginning of his street— I wasn't that much of a devil, but I wanted him to walk. I wanted him to stumble until he got to his house to realize we just broke up. I wanted him to hurt. And I wanted to keep on driving, until I was numb.

Jason

It was Saturday morning at 8 AM, and my mom was already pacing. I was at the table, finishing up some homework I started yesterday, so I could possibly hang out with Kennedy today. I still felt horrible for leaving her last night, and I was so mad that my mom and I got into this huge fight. Which made matters even worse because today was when the test results came back. Of course she was on edge all week, hell, I have been shaking non-stop.

"Mom, you have to sit down," I yawned.

"I'm too nervous," I grabbed her shoulders suddenly and pushed her down into a chair.

"And I'm getting sick of you pacing. Relax." I said, more for her than for me. Even though I was terrified as well.

"Fine then, distract me. You didn't even tell me about the girl last night. You just yelled about how that was horrible of me," She huffed like a kid. I chuckled at her adolescence act, and shook my head.

"She is my friend, and we just wanted to hang out," I replied.

"I thought friends were bullshit to you now, isn't that what you told me after you stopped talking to Harrison?" She questioned. I couldn't help but feel a stab of pain at his name.

"Yea, but she's—"

"Different?" She asked.

"No, not different. Better." I replied. My mom nodded her head slowly, and grinned at me suddenly. "I'm leaving if you keep looking at me like that."

"I'm just looking at you, what I can't look at my own son?"

"Not with that look!" I laughed.

"Oh, you mean the look that means I know you have a crush on that girl and you can't even admit it look, right?" She grinned brighter, and I rolled my eyes. I loved my mom like this, playful and relaxed. I wish it was like this all the time. A normal family, talking about normal things. I wish it was that easy, except suddenly the phone rang.

We both looked at each other, and the room started to get smaller. She looked scared, and I wanted to tell her everything was going to be okay, but even I wasn't sure. It rang for a third time before my mom picked it up. She didn't even say hello, she just gave a grunt of approval, most likely at the question of her name. I could feel my breathing stagger, with every second the person on the phone kept speaking. I gnawed on my lip, trying to believe in some sort of higher power to help me out here. I ran over possibilities in my mind: What if she was negative? What if she was positive? What would happen? How would she handle it? How would I handle it? What would happen to us?

I looked at my mom, her eyes fixed on the wood table. I didn't know what to do without her. She is the only family I ever had. She raised me all by herself, without any help from anyone. She was the strongest person I knew, and this is what she gets for all her hard work? I wanted to believe in a God, and maybe I did, but right now I didn't. Right now, I couldn't.

She finally gave a small thank you and goodbye, and then hung up. She looked at me with her big grey eyes, the same she gave to me. She gave me a sad, small smile and I felt my whole world crashing down in that moment. I put my head in my hands, and I couldn't stop the tears from escaping my body. In between sobs, I could hear her say

"It's going to be alright," but I knew she was trying to make me feel better. Nothing could make me feel better now.

❀

My mom kicked me out of the house for a couple of hours. She didn't want me to be in the house when she started packing all of her stuff. She also had to make some calls to Uncle Tim so he could come up and help us out for the time being. The only good news was that she would be situated in the local hospital thirty minutes away, so I could finish up my senior year without another issue. But it's not like that made it any easier.

However, instead of dreading on what just happened she literally pushed me out of the house and said "Find your girl." And that was that. She didn't even listen to me when I said that I didn't know where she lived. She just threw my keys at me, and slammed the door in my face. All in good intention I hope. My chest was still heavy, and my pessimism was at its height, but I pushed it to the back of my mind. I knew I wanted to see Kennedy, but I didn't know what I would say. She would obviously know something is wrong, because she always knows. That's what I love about her.

I groaned feeling so many emotions at once. I was terrified and depressed but nervous and eager. Feelings were bullshit, but that didn't stop me from feeling them. All the fucking time.

I decided to call her. Part of me hoping she'd pick up, part of me hoping she wouldn't.

"Hi," I said when the receiver on the other end picked up.

"Jason? Is everything okay?" How does she always know?

"Yea... kinda, I mean— do you want to go somewhere with me?" I asked horribly.

"Want me to meet you somewhere?" She asked, and I could hear the smile in her voice.

"I could just pick you up," I responded.

"Um...I don't know if that's...a good idea," she seemed uneasy.

"Why, do you secretly need permission from your mom too?" I teased.

"Something like that," she laughed. I could practically hear the gears in her head turning. "Okay, I'll text you my address. But, promise you'll tell me what's wrong before you ask me anything."

"Deal, I'll see you soon," I replied, trying to hide my eagerness.

"I'll see you," and she hung up. I knew I was fucked up for being mildly happy on a day like this, but maybe thats why my mom sent me out today. Embarrassing, but I still love her. I didn't even tell her much, and she knew I already liked Kennedy. She knew before I did. I didn't know whether to hate her for that, or love her.

It's not like I wanted to ask her out then and there, but I just wanted to be with her. She made me feel like I wasn't Bullshit Boy anymore, either that, or she accepted me. She didn't look at me like I was crazy either. She also was beautiful in all she is, and always asks the right questions. It's hard to find someone who always asks the right questions— so when you find them, don't let them go. And I don't intend on letting Kennedy go that easily.

I received her text message soon after, and I opened it to put it into the navigation system. Though my heart

71

dropped in the pit of my stomach for the second time today, and it was only 9 AM.

Kennedy

I thought I would have more time with him before he found out I was Harrison's sister. I thought he could get to know me better, and I him. So when I told him, he wouldn't despise me. But, from what things are looking like, today was the day. Harrison was also leaving, he didn't tell me where he was going, but by the time he walks out of the house Jason would be there waiting for me. Probably confused, and probably pissed.

But I really hope Jason will keep his promise, and tell me what was bothering him. Just one word from him, and I knew. I didn't know how, but something told me he needed me today.

"Who was that?" Harrison asked after I hung up the phone.

"My friend. He's picking me up soon so we can hang out," I replied slowly.

"A guy friend?" Harrison perked.

"You know him," I responded carefully.

"I do?" Harrison asked more to himself. "I don't see you hanging around any of my friends?"

"I didn't say he was your friend," I replied, as I looked uneasily towards Harrison. He was biting into an apple in deep thought. "You didn't tell me where you were going," I started.

"August asked if I wanted to have breakfast," he smiled to himself. "Don't hate me okay," he quickly added.

"I don't hate you for hanging out with her. Actually, I'm glad you are," I responded. Harrison suddenly coughed and took quick breath.

"Wait, what? Since when? I thought you hated her," Harrison stated.

73

"I did before because you were heads over heels for a girl who never really paid you any attention. But now that she is… I don't know, maybe she actually likes you," I honestly replied. Harrison was speechless, and I rolled my eyes at his dumb reaction. "Oh come on, even I noticed she hangs out with you more than her said boyfriend."

"Don't give me false hope."

"I'm not, I'm stating a fact. Do what you will with it. Just be careful… she always seems to have a secret agenda," I reminded him.

"I know…but so do you," he retorted. I gave him a icy glare and he grinned at me like an ass.

"Hey, so…when this guy comes," I started again, "Please, don't do anything irrational. Just hear me out, and hear him out, and then be angry or be stoic, okay?"

"Do you like him?" I heard him ask, but I started to get my coat on. "Oh my god," he continued. "Holy fuck, Kennedy!"

"I'm going to hit you if you keep making this a big deal," I replied coldly.

"What? Are you kidding? My little baby sister has a crush— I was starting to think you didn't feel anything," Harrison ran over to me and picked me up in a bear hug. "Now you can understand how I feel with August,".

"Oh god no. I don't love him, I don't even know that much about him. I just…really like him that's all," Harrison smirked at me and I groaned uncomfortably, "I don't look at him like he's the reason I'm alive, like someone I know," I snarked, yet Harrison just rolled his eyes.

"I'm excited," He said. "Should we tell the parents that you were surprisingly born with a heart?"

"Let them sleep, they've been busy the whole week. Just, promise me okay… don't make this a big deal. And whatever happens…don't hate me," I pleaded.

"I couldn't hate you Ken, even if you did something really shitty, I'm sure I'll get over it."

"Please, keep that in mind," I replied as I felt a vibration in my pocket. Jason texted me that he was here and I knew it was time for D-Day.

Harrison

I woke up with my phone ringing and August's name on my screen. It wasn't my ideal way of waking up, but it was something good.

"Hello?" My voice was rough from sleep as I picked up the phone.

"Shit, did I wake you up?" August's voice slipped underneath my skin.

"Yea, but I don't mind," I smiled to myself, "Is something wrong?"

"No…yea, well…do you want to get breakfast with me? I know this great diner on route 306, I think you'd like it." Today was going to be a good day, I called it. I never thought August's voice would wake me up ever, but here we are. And I love it with every fiber of my being.

"Yea, sure," I cleared my throat, "When should I pick you up?"

"Umm… I'm out right now, so I'll just meet you there. How does 11:30 sound? I know it's late, but…" She trailed off and I felt like flying.

"Yea, that's perfect. Send me the address and I'll see you," I replied happily.

"Sure, I'll see you soon," And with that the receiver hung up and I couldn't help myself from my excitement.

I got ready in five minutes flat. To say I was eager as hell was an understatement. All I knew was that I wanted to be with her, even if that means being her friend. I just wanted to hear her laugh, and see her smile everyday. I want to be the first one to hear which college she got into, and her aspirations. I want to know her fears, and make sure she faces each one head on. I want her to think of me, and smile. That's all I want.

I don't know if that's love, or something like that but I won't deny what I feel. I'll just be there for her, and hope she does the same for me.

I rushed downstairs and grabbed an apple, while Kennedy was at the counter speaking on the phone. Once she hung up, I took a quick bite.

"Who was that?" I asked, chewing. She fiddled with her phone before answering.

"My friend. He's picking me up soon so we can hang out." She replied slowly, as if she was afraid of my reaction.

"A guy friend?" I asked, making her fidget. Could it be that my little sister has a crush? *Oh... this is so good.*

"You know him," She responded. My eyebrows raised in shock.

"I do?" I asked, thinking of all the guys on my soccer team. I swear, I never saw her with any of them, "I don't see you hanging around any of my friends?"

"I didn't say he was your friend," she replied, her voice lowering. Holy shit, maybe she really did like this guy. "You didn't tell me where you were going," she said, changing the subject. She *totally* likes this guy.

"August asked if I wanted to have breakfast," I grinned, but stopped myself knowing Kennedy too well, "Don't hate me okay," she rolled her eyes in response.

"I don't hate you for hanging out with her. Actually, I'm glad you are," I choked on my apple and my eyes almost fell out of my head in shock. Kennedy always does this thing where she says something you thought you'd never hear. Like right now.

"Wait, what?" I tried getting the piece of apple down my throat, "Since when? I thought you hated her?"

"I did before because you were heads over heels for a girl who never really paid you any attention. But now that she is… I don't know, maybe she actually likes you," I couldn't help my mouth from dropping at this revolution. "Oh come on, even I noticed she hangs out with you more than her said boyfriend." Could it be? No, I couldn't think like that.

"Don't give me false hope," I replied, trying to ease my brain.

"I'm not, I'm stating a fact. Do what you will with it. Just be careful… she always seems to have a secret agenda," she reminded me, but I already knew.

"I know…but so do you," I replied back, and she gave me a cold stare. I had to grin at her, nothing could hide my happiness this morning. I watched as she played with her shirt and her hair before speaking again.

"Hey so…when this guy comes," she started carefully, "Please, don't do anything irrational. Just hear me out, and hear him out, and then be angry or be stoic, okay?" She pleaded. Now I just had to ask, she was practically easing me into it.

"Do you like him?" I whispered. She looked at the ground and started to get her coat from the coat closet. "Oh my god," I realized, "Holy fuck, Kennedy!"

"I'm going to hit you if you keep making this a big deal," she snapped as she shrugged her coat on.

"What? Are you kidding? My little baby sister has a crush — I was starting to think you didn't feel anything," I whooped and ran over to pick her up in a bear hug, oozing happiness for my little baby sister. "Now you can understand what I feel with August," I added.

"Oh god no. I don't love him, I don't even know that much about him. I just…really like him thats all. I don't

78

look at him like he's the reason I'm alive, like someone I know," she teased as she eased out of my grasp. I let her go, and took another bite of my apple still happy for her.

"I'm excited," I grinned brightly. "Should we tell the parents that you were surprisingly born with a heart?" I teased as she laughed and rolled her eyes.

"Let them sleep, they've been busy this whole week. Just, promise me okay... don't make this a big deal. And whatever happens... don't hate me," I was confused at Kennedy's fear. Did she think I was going to embarrass her that bad?

"I couldn't hate you Ken, even if you did something really shitty, I'm sure I'll get over it," I reassured her.

"Please, keep that in mind," She clenched her jaw as her phone binged with a text. She took a big breath and stared at the door as if she was wondering if it was worth it or not. I shook my head at her. I never seen this side of her before, it was cute. I laughed and decided to open the door by myself. As I opened the door, she screamed wait. But it was too late.

Emily

"Will you please sit down, Emily," Kerrey, my lovely and annoyed therapist groaned again. I was pacing, as I usually do, around her office. Sitting in that damn blue chair that everyone sits in and whines about their problems instead of doing something about them, bothers me. So, I make it my mission to not sit down in that phony chair. Instead, I walk around. Pace, sometimes. And when I'm really in a good mood, I sit in Kerrey's chair. "You're wasting my time," Kerrey pushed.

"Shouldn't you be asking — *Emily, why are you in such a good mood? What have you accomplished this week? Any new epiphanies and such?*" I recited in my best Kerrey voice. From the corner of my eye, I saw a small smile reach her face. I also smiled to myself, and waited for her to respond.

"Why are you in such a good mood Emily?" She smiled, playing along. I sighed, and ran my hand over the many books, she probably never read, on her shelf.

"Oh where to begin?," I exasperated, "I am leaving in less than a month, I'm slowly learning how to beat Woodstock in chess, Sam's mother gets to come out to the activity room today, the nineteenth of next month, and today Robyn is making pumpkin pie and I'm so fucking excited," I sighed and waited for her input. She did the therapist-once-over-look, trying to decipher the hidden meanings behind my words before answering.

"Two questions, which one would you like first: the one that will make you wonder, or the one that will make you scared?" Kerrey asked carefully. I made my way to the wall adjacent of the bookshelf, where all of Kerrey's certificates and degrees hang in vanity.

"I guess, the one that will make me scared," I replied quietly, starting to become terrified of her question.

"Do you enjoy Sam?" I had to laugh at her sudden question.

"Enjoy him? He's not some toy I prefer out of all the others, Kerrey. He's my friend...the first one I have in a while," I replied, still not making eye contact.

"Do you like him? More than a friend, of course," she asked, with no hesitation.

"Is that question supposed to scare me? Of course I like him, I have to if I actually call him a friend," I answered, scrutinizing her degree from Columbia.

"You're not answering the question."

"I am."

"Never once have you mentioned a friend here, and now you mention this boy Sam. Everyone here knows you both have a bond, and you are telling me that you don't have any feelings for this boy... at all?" Kerrey pushed again.

"I'm a fucked up girl Kerrey, and Sam is surrounded by fucked up people...I don't want to be fucked up if it means...ya know...being with him," I stuttered stupidly, hoping she understood what I meant.

"Do you think you're getting better?" I bit my lip with her question, and turned to look at her. She looked at ease, with her right leg resting upon her left, and a pad and pencil in her hand; like she's done this a thousand times.

"I hope so. I hope all of these months can be successful of something. I obviously am different from who I once was...but I don't really know if that's a good thing or not," I responded honestly.

"You have made a difference from your time here, but the person who must find out if it's better comes down to you," She added.

"Well...I know the person I was put me in here in the first place. The person I was allowed people to step all over her, and made her parents worry, and made everyone annoyed. And the person I am, makes people mad, and makes my parents embarrassed, and doesn't allow people to walk over me at all. How can I see if that's better? I'm so fucked up, I don't even know..." I chuckled at the irony of it, and hated that I couldn't figure myself out.

"The way you see if you did get better is the people around you now. The people who are around you now know you as you are, the changed you. Do you think these people are better than the people who you used to know? Are they worth it?" Kerrey explained as she looked at me. I didn't know if she really did care about me. Hell, do any therapists actually care about their clients or their client's money? But the fact that she is talking with me, the fact that she actually acts like she cares, makes her better than most.

"The way I see your question is, was it worth sacrificing August and all of those shit people for Sam and everyone who really cares for me now... and that's a definite 700% yes. It was completely worth it, and I would make that sacrifice in every life I will ever live wholeheartedly," I replied confidently.

Kerrey smiled at me, and nodded her head. "Then, I can say that you did get better. Now are you ready for your next question?" I sat myself on the wooden table in front of that annoyingly blue chair, and nodded my head.

"Are you ready to go out there?" Kerrey asked, and I knew she was talking about the real world. Was I ready to tell people where I've been, and explain to them that I'm not the same, fragile piece of shit they used to know? The big, lovely question daunted by every person in here. Was I ready for it?

I looked down at my untied laces of my old Nike's and sighed. "I'll do my best."

"Explain, please," Kerrey's skeptical eyebrow raised.

"I mean, whether I'm ready or not for the unpredictable and absolutely terrifying real world, I will try my best. That's what everyone does anyway," I replied hoping for the best. Kerrey smiled at me and closed her pad, and placed her pencil down on the desk. She stood, and stretched out her hand, and gave me on of her even-though-I'm-a-therapist-I-am-still-a-human look.

"I believe we are finished here."

Jason

I pulled up to the generic brick house with the two wind chimes on the front porch and tried not to feel anything. It looked exactly how it did all the times I pulled up to this house before. It didn't change a bit, not even the faded carvings on the front white porch, with my name in it. I clenched my jaw, and wondered why the hell Kennedy asked me to come here. I tried to get every possible thought out of my head, because assuming things are bullshit. But that didn't mean I was fucking confused, and fucking pissed. Just more emotions to add to the list.

I walked out of my car, and texted Kennedy that I was here. I made my way to the passenger side of my car, and leaned on the door waiting. Hoping she would come out of the house to the right or the left. But also a part of me hoping that Harrison would come out, and see me. Probably confused as me.

A part of me always wanted to talk to him again, and tell him I'm sorry for all the shit I did. But I also wanted him to say sorry too, for not asking me why, and caring that I left. We were best friends since we were kids, and even though people leave all the time, I prayed that he wouldn't. Yet, it was my fault. Telling him of all the bullshit he had, I wished he would've listened. I wish it was different. But wishing the past was different is the dumb bullshit people wish for all the time. All we can do now is hope for the best.

Suddenly, the door opened and all I could hear was Kennedy scream. My head snapped up, and I found myself running toward the door only to stop in my tracks.

"Holy fuck," I whispered to myself. I couldn't decide if this was my worst nightmare, or one of the dreams I didn't

84

dare to confess. Harrison stared at me, with Kennedy frantically looking between us. Harrison looked at me, and then turned to Kennedy, his brows furrowing trying to figure out how this makes sense.

"Jason. That's the guy," Harrison asked, clenching his teeth. Her eyes searched his, while I tried to search hers. *Was this her plan all along?*

"I-I was gonna tell you. I promise you, I wanted to. You too," She looked at me and her eyes were brimming with tears, "I just...you two need each other and I hated the way you both became after. Harrison, you are in love with someone who doesn't love you back, and you can't accept that. And Jason...you pushed everyone who loved you away. Don't you see that you need each other, and don't you feel like shit because you both just gave up."

I looked at Harrison, who didn't stop glaring at Kennedy. I wanted to hate her. I wanted to start my fucking car and leave that place. I wanted to never talk to either one of them ever again. I wanted to forget I ever knew the names Kennedy and Harrison. But something held me to my place. Maybe it was the way Harrison looked at me: with anger, confusion, and hurt. Or maybe it was the way Kennedy stared at me: just asking me, pleading me, to stay.

"You've got to be fucking kidding me, Kennedy. Jason was the guy you're talking about. The house you went to when I was losing my mind trying to find you, the one you've been hanging out with, the fucking guy you like.... Jason," Harrison spoke out loud, as if he was trying to convince himself this was real. I looked to Kennedy, and before she could stop them, tears flowed down her face as she bit her lip. The girl who I thought was invincible, and couldn't figure out, was crying for me. Well, half for me. But nevertheless, the girl I reluctantly like so fucking much, was crying. And even when I wanted to hate her, and yell at her and just leave, I couldn't leave her there. Something in me just couldn't. I was already, possibly, losing my mother. And the very thought of losing Kennedy killed me. "Did you know about this?" Harrison suddenly asked. I shook my head, clenching my jaw.

"I didn't know she was your sister," I found myself saying, colder than I intended.

"I know you didn't really talk to her when we were friends, but for fuck sake Jason, she's my fucking sister," Harrison exclaimed.

"You don't think I've realized that?" I shouted.

"No, I'm sure your bullshit defense mechanism makes you realize most things these days," Harrison snapped.

"You know what Harrison, it does. I can actually care for someone, and know that they care for me instead of being in fucking love with someone who doesn't even know when your birthday is," I shot back without hesitation.

The next thing I knew, Harrison was running toward me while Kennedy started screaming in the background. I felt his hard knuckles connect with my jaw before I could register what happened. I felt the pain only when I fell to the ground. I spit the blood out of my mouth, and looked at Harrison as he held me by the collar of my shirt. I expected his eyes to be burning with sparks shooting out of them, but they were red with sadness instead. I always knew he loved August, but before I left him, he never really showed it. I felt bad for the way I treated him, but I wasn't the only one at fault.

"Harrison! Get off of him!" Kennedy pushed Harrison of of me, and put her hands on my face, searching for any wounds. Her tears fell on my shirt and face, and I could hear her whisper I'm sorry over and over again. I sat up, and looked at Harrison who was sitting across from me.

We stayed there for a few minutes, trying to wonder how this is going to work, or if it even was worth fixing. I noticed Harrison stir as he looked on the ground in front of him, and I followed his eyes to a crushed up cigarette on the floor.

"You kept it," Harrison stuttered as he found my eyes again.

"I promised that I would," I responded, wiping my mouth with my sleeve.

"I thought you would throw it away, or hell, start again," Harrison chuckled.

I shook my head, "Cigarettes are bullshit. This one isn't though."

"Why the fuck did you keep it?"

I groaned as I stretched to get the ruined cigarette in front of us. I straightened it and inspected my very last cigarette. "Why the fuck do you think I kept it?"

"What happened to you?" Harrison sighed and ran a hand through his hair. I remembered, in that moment, how it was before. Before my mom started getting the signs. Before I lost money to pay for my college tuition. Before I realized all the bullshit. Back to days where Harrison and I planned a future where we were comrades till death. Back to the days where I had friends, and something to do every day. Back to the days when I wasn't Bullshit Boy.

"So much shit."

"That's not an excuse."

"I'm not using it as an excuse," I snapped, "I just couldn't… handle everything."

"You didn't have to do it by yourself Jason. You helped me when my parents were thinking of divorcing. You were there when my uncle died. You were there for all of it, and all I wanted was to be there for you man," Harrison pushed.

"There were so many times—"

"I know, me too," Harrison nodded.

"My mom's moving into the hospital in a few days," I took a deep breath before I could start again, "…. she has cancer,".

"Oh my god," Kennedy put her hands to her mouth.

"Fuck Jason," Harrison ran his hair though his hair and shook his head.

"It's okay…I've been emotionally trying to accept this for a long time. She's just all I've got…" I choked.

"You have us," Kennedy squeezed my hand, and I looked at her beautiful face, and I knew I was already in too deep. I looked to Harrison, who gave me one of his one sided smirks.

And I knew it was going to be okay. Even if there was worse to come, I knew it was going to be okay.

Kennedy

I hope Jason didn't know my hands were shaking. This was not the way I intended to see him today— but it ended better than I first intended. I waited in Jason's car, as Jason and Harrison talked outside. I could only make a few words, but they hugged at the end and I think everything was going to be okay, at least for now. But that's all I can hope for. That's all anyone can hope for.

Jason slid into his car, and I saw Harrison wave us off awkwardly as we went off. I played with my fingers knowing that this wasn't over yet. The air was so dense, I had to crack my window a little to even breathe.

"Was this your plan from the beginning?" Jason asked, breaking the silence.

"It was at first…but not now," I answered quietly. He nodded his head slowly, keeping his eyes on the road.

"So was it a success? Did you get what you wanted?" Jason asked and I didn't know if it was meant to sting the way it did. "It's okay if you say yes," Jason added, "Sure, I'm pissed at you, but I could be more angry if what you did was solely for yourself. You pretend to be my friend so you can help your brother and I in the end…and the only reason that Harrison and I are going to start over is because of you. So, I have to thank you because of that."

"I didn't pretend to be your friend, and I'm not pretending that I like you either," I stated stronger than I thought I did.

"Just making sure," Jason slowly smiled and I punched his shoulder in annoyance. He laughed and rubbed the spot where I punched him.

"Tell me about that cigarette, what's so special about it anyway?" I asked, my curiosity getting the best of me.

"I knew you would ask me sooner or later, you just can't help yourself," Jason glanced over at me, and his warm gaze made me glow. "Ironically, I used to smoke. I started in middle school, and stopped the summer going into my junior year. Harrison was sick of it, and hated that I had that habit. He always used to tell me that I was going to regret it when we become professional soccer players. I didn't listen to him, until your uncle died from tuberculosis. Harrison saw what he went through, and he didn't want to see the same thing happen to me. So, he threw away all my cigarettes, and sold off the guys who sold me them. Hell, he even took my wallet for a whole two months until he could trust me again. But he gave me one last cigarette and told me that this was the last cigarette I will ever have in my possession. He said that I could either smoke it now or save it for a day when I need it. But either or, this cigarette was the last one. And even if I don't smoke it or I do, when I finally finish my last cigarette, and I am down to the very end of it, he would still be there," Jason smiled at the warm memory, and I smiled with him. "I don't really know why I kept it. It just feels weird not to have it with me."

"Don't worry, I understand," I replied. He glanced at me and smiled.

"I know you do."

"Where are we going?" I asked, feeling the nervousness slip through my window crack.

"My favorite spot in the whole world…so far," Jason responded.

"Wait, I have a question," I said without thinking. He laughed as he turned onto the highway.

"Of course you do… go for it."

"Are you bullshit boy? Now, I mean," I asked, hoping he wouldn't get angry. He took a big breath, and I saw him thinking about my words.

"I think bullshit boy will always be a part of me, but I don't think I'm fully him anymore," Jason answered. "I think I'm both Jason and bullshit boy."

"So, when you're not being bullshit boy, I'll call you Jason. And when you are—,"

"Nope, you cannot call me bullshit boy. Absolutely not," Jason shook his head immediately.

"Then what can I call you when you're not being Jason?" I pouted.

"Jason," I laughed as his abrupt answer.

"You're not fun."

"And you're really cute when you don't get your way. Maybe, we should make that a daily thing," Jason teased.

I blushed and punched his shoulder again pretending that I was angry. But, in that moment, I couldn't remember when I was happier. The window barely cracked, the radio on a low hum, the open road before us, and Jason's hand slowly finding mine.

Harrison

I walked quickly into the diner on route 306. It had a red and metallic theme, and most people who were here at this hour were old couples on dates. I scanned the diner, and my eyes caught her. I immediately knew something was wrong. August was looking out the window, watching the cars on the highway pass by, her eyes getting sadder each time they fell out of view. Her jaw was clenched, and her hair was thrown in a ponytail, which is not an August thing to do. She just looked ultimately sad, and all I wanted to do was make her feel better.

I walked toward her, and once I got close enough she snapped her head up to me. Her dim face, brightened a bit as she smiled at me.

"Harrison, I was worried you weren't coming," she chuckled, playing her mug of hot tea.

"I always will," I replied, not thinking, and realizing how fucking weird that sounded like. "I was caught up with some thing with Kennedy, and surprisingly, Jason," I honestly added.

"Bullshit boy? What happened?" She asked, intrigued.

"Well, remember when Jason and I were best friends?" I started.

"No way…I mean, I remember but…. that was so long ago," She responded.

"Yea, well…he and Kennedy are kind of together," I smiled feeling so fucking awkward about it.

"Oh my god, are you serious? Your best friend and your sister…holy shit Harrison," she laughed and my heart swelled because I could make her do that.

"Yea, it's weird as fuck. But they are happy…and I'm actually really glad Jason is coming back into my life. It sounds cheesy, but he was my best friend. He still is. I need him," I smiled and shook my head, having a hard time believing all of this went down this morning.

"I'm glad, I'm really happy for you then, everyone needs someone even if they can't admit it," her smile this time was sad, and I couldn't stop myself from asking her.

"Are you okay? Why did you ask me out to here? Is something wrong, August?" I asked, worried for her answer. Her smile faded and she kept eye contact with her tea while sighing.

"I broke up with Kevin last night," she said, and my mouth dropped.

"Oh fuck, are you okay?" I asked, hating that I felt a little bit happy.

"Honestly, I'm fine. I'm worried about him. I left him on the sidewalk after I broke up with him in my car," she replied and my mouth dropped.

"August! Seriously?" I smiled a bit, thinking how funny it would've been. "I didn't know you were like that," I joked.

"Of course you didn't know I was like that. You don't know anything about me," her voice grew cold, and my smile faded immediately. I wanted to ask what was really wrong, but for some reason my mouth couldn't form words. I just watched her clench her jaw even more, and her eyes start to water. Her gaze suddenly snapped to me and I think my heart broke. "Oh, for fuck sake Harrison, stop looking at me like that!" She exclaimed.

"Like what?" I heard my voice whisper.

"Like I am the very reason you're here on this earth. Like I'm your fucking gravity. Like you would die for me, stop looking at me like that," She spat, a tear falling over her bottom lashes. I started to shake my head, but she gave a cold laugh. "Don't act like you don't know what I'm talking about. The whole world probably already knows that you love me. Hell, I knew. I've known for the longest time, and only now it's bothering me," Her voice started to choke up, and she tried to calm herself down. "You have no idea who I am, Harrison. You have no idea what I've done to people to get my way. I can't sit here and have you believe I'm some angel. I'm as fucked up as the next person, and probably even more. I've done so many bad things, I can't even live with myself. And you…you, Harrison don't deserve someone as horrible as me. I mean, God… you are magnificent. You're intelligent, and funny, and pure, and so fucking beautiful…and I can't have you love me. You can't love me Harrison." She wiped the tears that fell down her face with an angry hand and waited for my answer.

I just looked at her, the girl who I loved for the longest time, cry for me. I always knew that she knew I loved her, but hear her saying it didn't feel as good as I hoped it would've. I had to digest everything she just said before speaking.

"I knew that you weren't an angel… I didn't expect an angel. I expected you, and I wanted to get to know you. Why is that so bad?" I asked, my voice getting harder as well.

"Because you love me already. You can't love me, no one can love me, that's just the unsaid, and unwritten rule. You can't love me and not know anything about me."

"Just being with—,"

"Stop, Harrison. I knew you loved me, and that's why I asked you to help me. I needed to get to know you, so I could find a way to turn you away. I already read most of Bukowski's books, and I love Salinger. I didn't need help at all, I just needed to understand you. I needed to understand why the fuck you could fall so hard for someone like me. But that's the thing, you can't. Don't you get it Harrison? I'm trying to help you here, you're too good for me. You deserve better," she cut in, hoping to make her point.

"So, all of it was a lie?" I responded, feeling my blood boil. "I've already been lied to by my sister and my best friend today, so just fucking tell me."

"Most of it, I did want to help you find your sister and I do like…being with you Harrison— but you're not the problem. What you feel for me, is the problem." She explained. I shook my head, my breathing getting faster. "Oh come on Harrison, no one can glow and be happy all the time, people who believe I'm like that are fools."

"I didn't want you to pretend to glow or be happy, I just wanted you to be with me," I clenched my teeth.

"You love me better and harder than anyone I have ever seen. That's why I can't fool you. That's why I can't let you love me. Haven't you realized I'm a horrible person… I fucking put someone in the hospital Harrison. You don't know anything about my life and what I've done. You can't possibly love someone like that, and I won't let you. You deserve someone as pure as you, with gold intentions and a warm heart. You deserve someone not as fucked up as me, and can love you harder than you love them. I'm not that person, and I will never be."

"Don't fucking tell me what I deserve, August. Sure, I don't know you, but you don't know me either. Why should that stop me from feeling the way I do. I can't fucking help it okay, you have no idea how many times I wanted to stop loving you. But I couldn't and I can't, and you're just going to have to get used to it," I snapped.

"People like you and me can never love each other, no matter how many times you sell your soul to the devil, we can never be together," She broke eye contact, more of her tears falling on the table.

"Why not?" I said matching her lower volume.

"Have you ever seen an angel and devil fall for each other, and end up fine?" I searched her red, sad eyes for the answer. "That's why," she picked up her bag and left a five dollar bill on the table. I wanted to hold her hand, yell at her some more, and make her stay. But I was frozen. She stood up and looked at me, more tears falling from her eyes. She put my face in both of her hands and placed a soft kiss on my forehead. "I wish things were different — I wish *I* was different... I'm so sorry, Harrison," She pulled back and looked into my eyes, giving me the saddest smile I've ever seen. "Thank you for loving me."

Then she left.

Emily

I immediately started screaming once she made her final move and smiled innocently at Woodstock.

"Checkmate," she smiled as Woodstock's mouth dropped wide open, and while I was still in screaming-victory mode.

"Holy fuck you did it! You did the fucking impossible!" I shouted, still in shock. Rebecca laughed at Woodstock's unbelievable face. I wrapped my arms around Rebecca and started laughing at Woodstock too. "You are my hero. You have no idea how many times I've tried and failed. But here you are, first time player, and you beat the king," I added.

"Beginners luck I guess?" Rebecca shrugged easily.

"More like winners touch," I smirked at Woodstock. He growled at me, and cleared his throat.

"I think my glasses were a bit foggy, I also am under the weather—,"

"Shut your pie hole Woodstock, and admit defeat old man," I cut in. He glared at me, with a smirk twitching his lips. He rolled his eyes and shook Rebecca's hand. He grumbled once again and slowly started to get out of his loser chair. I quickly took his place and gave Rebecca a bright grin. "See, I told you there was nothing to be afraid of. Everyone is technically harmless,". Rebecca showed me a small smile and shrugged once again.

"I'm just not use to places like this... I didn't really know what to expect," She confessed.

"I know the first day in here is pretty daunting, but trust me, in a couple of days you'll feel better. And if you don't, I'm always here," I responded wholeheartedly. She took my hand in hers and looked at me with eyes like Sam's.

"Thank you for everything…f or being here and helping me, and my son," Her eyes watered, and I pulled my hands away from hers.

"What did I say about the tears! No tears, I don't do tears," I exclaimed trying to keep the room bright. She sniffled and gave me one of her signature smiles.

Rebecca came out this morning, and you could literally feel her fear from the other side of the room. I knew she was Sam's mom because of her eyes. They were identical to Sam's, who is coming soon to check on his mom's first day.

Though, she was scared at first, once I told her of who I was and that I knew Sam, she immediately relaxed. The whole day I've been showing her around the place, and introducing her to everyone that was worth knowing. And seeing her beat Woodstock was the best thing that could've happened to me today.

I also had a revelation today as well. While showing Rebecca around, it finally hit me that I was leaving. I know that I haven't been here for that long, but before felt like another life. Another person. Yet, now I know who I am and where I'm going— at least where I want to go. I am leaving all these people, and only Lord knows if I'll ever see them again. And though that is sad for me, I know that I'm going back into the world (which is completely fucking terrifying) and starting over again. Just trying life again, and hoping to get it right this time.

From seeing where I came from, to where I am now, to where I'm headed, it all seems like a dream. All the people that badly affected my life in some way are just faces in the background, and the people that greatly affected my life are here, right now, with me. And it feels so good to see them smiling, and to smile myself and not feel guilty about it.

I know of the possibilities of relapse out there, but I also know my own will power to be better. Not only for myself, but for the people around me. For the people that matter to me.

I heard a distant familiar voice and a smile found my lips instantly. I turned to see Sam walking toward us with a smile, and his hands in his pockets. His hair was damp, just like the first day he stumbled into my hospital room.

"Seems like you two are getting along," he grinned as he pulled a chair up.

"Of course we are, she just beat *the* Woodstock at chess and I will forever look up to her for that," I grinned back. Sam looked at his mom and held her hand. They didn't need to say anything, they just knew.

"How are you?" He asked to Rebecca and she looked at me when she responded.

"Better than I hoped, thanks to your beautiful friend here. Though her mouth is a bit dirty, I do appreciate everything she has done for me, and will do for me. I try to give my thanks, but she won't allow it," She huffed as a typical annoyed mother. I laughed at her choice of words and tucked a strand of hair behind my ear.

"The dirty mouth will never change, I am not sorry to say, and so is trying to give me thanks. There is no need," I shrugged off. Sam smirked at me and I stuck my tongue out at him playfully.

"I don't think you could even try to change Emily, not like I ever would though," I flicked his nose, rolling my eyes at his warming, yet cheesy remark. Rebecca laughed at us and smiled happily.

Suddenly, the bell for our daily dose of pills rang and I told Rebecca where to go to get hers. I was put off mine thanks to Dr. Kerrey. Wonderful woman she is.

"I'm happy you like her," Sam said once Rebecca was out of hearing distance.

"How could I not, she's like you, but female, older, and motherly," I joked.

"I mean, we both know how much you like me, but fail to say it," My eyes widened at him, "Don't worry, I'll keep your secret. I feel the same anyway," I felt my face heat up, and I made sure not to make eye contact with him. "But we'll wait for the nineteenth," I chuckled and rolled my eyes.

"Yes, the nineteenth," I smiled at him.

"Are you nervous about going back to school?" He suddenly asked, changing the subject. I sighed and bit my lip while thinking.

"I guess...I would be lying if I said I wasn't. It's not that I'm afraid of the classes and starting late, I can handle that, it's the people. I can handle many now, but not that many. Especially, a particular girl. But I'll try... that's all I can do. Don't get me wrong, I'm happy to be getting out of here, but sad I have to leave as well. It's so weird to be leaving all these amazing people. Like your mom, and Dr. Kerrey, and Robyn— ugh I'll miss her cooking, and Woodstock— even though I don't show it, I love Woodstock, and you. Mostly you," I responded honestly.

"I have a car, and a license Emily. You don't have to miss me," he replied. "You've helped me in so many ways, you don't even understand. I know you look at yourself as this damaged goods type of girl, but you've got it wrong. I can't stress enough how wrong you've got it."

I looked at Sam and felt his hand find mine. Though the weight of the world hasn't lifted itself off my shoulders, and there were so many unknowns, what if's, maybes, and

why's left— I knew it was going to be okay from then on. I
was positive.

August

Their laughs muffled as I saw Harrison from across the field, sitting underneath a tree with Bullshit Boy— Jason now, I assume. I couldn't stop my chest from burning and breaking my rib cage with every beat of my tainted heart. Yet, I still laughed along to whatever the people I was sitting with were making a joke of. Most likely about someones outfit, or something that they said. Shit like that.

"I still find it so weird that you and Kevin broke up, we all thought you guys were getting practically married," Laura pushed my shoulder slightly, feigning a pout.

"It was pretty mutual, honestly," I shrugged, and flashed my best smile, "We both knew that college was coming up, and we both needed to branch out. He will always be in my heart though," the girls put their hands to their hearts and awed, saying how they wished they were as mature as me, and that they had a relationship like I had.

Fucking pathetic.

I couldn't help my eyes from finding Harrison. I missed the way he smiled and it fucking killed me. I knew I shouldn't, I couldn't— but here we are. The boy in love, finally out, and the girl who never loves, falling to a crash and burn. I almost rolled my eyes.

"August, you have to tell me your secret for perfect skin!" Some other girl whined to me. I gave her a bright smile, and let my glow radiate.

"Of course! Remind me to text you, but I have to go talk to my teacher about the statistics project," I wrapped up my lunch, chucked it into the trash, and left— but not without flashing my best smile back at them.

I suddenly couldn't feel my lungs, it was like the whole world was sitting on top of my chest, telling me to take deeper breaths as if it was an easy task. It was all so suffocating, and the only one I could breathe with was Harrison.

He's far better without me though, and in a couple of years he will come back and say thank you for getting him out of his deathly infatuation. I know he will meet this beautiful girl, who thinks with the purity of her heart. I know he will wonder *where have you been all my life?* I know everything from here on out will get better... for him.

My time has passed, and time doesn't give more minutes or hours or days for specific people. Time doesn't give a fuck about anyone. Especially someone like me. Someone who wasted her time with people who didn't deserve it.

Walking down the hallway, I saw Kevin out of the corner of my eye. I thought he was going to come running back, and start vomiting apologies one after the other, but he just smiled my way. One of those nostalgic smiles, that spoke novels. The type of novels I chose not to read. I gave him a small smile back (a real one), and continued on my way. Maybe it was too embarrassing to talk to me and it was just easier to accept the fact that we were over. He was a good guy, at the very least. He probably will find someone in his Junior year of college, because Lord knows it's going to take two years to get the traces of fuck-boy out out of him.

People gave me their best knock out smiles as I walked down the hallway, and I gave them really shitty ones in return. All I was thinking in that moment was how much longer I had to keep doing this, until I was free from their binding assumptions of who I am. College, was the home plate — the place where I can just strip off this uncomfortable skin of who they think is August. I didn't tell anyone where I was going, hell, I even lied. Everyone thought I was going to the state school, just like everyone pretty much did. Yet, I was a world away, and my excitement couldn't hide itself any longer. I can finally not hurt anyone around me anymore, and hopefully forget everyone. Especially, Harrison. He is definitely one of my biggest regrets and what if's at the same time. Yet, he'll never know.

I know that the usual stuff will never change, my dad will still go on his business trips, my mom will be wherever she is now, my brother still in the bottom of some lake, and I still wanting to be far away as ever. But I also know that theres so many opportunities in front of me. Maybe even, one day someone can hurt me as bad I used to hurt everyone. Maybe I'll fall for them. Maybe I won't. Maybe I fuck up again, or maybe I get better.

I sighed at the my abundance of maybes, and held onto my sliver of hope for a better tomorrow.

What else is a girl named after a month supposed to do anyway?

Jason

I lifted the black duffle bag onto the sofa near the
window, and watched as the midday traffic took its time to
get on the nearest highway. I heard Kennedy sigh next to
me, as she placed another piece of luggage near the sofa.

"I think thats it," she huffed, and I chuckled at her red
face.

"Oh, this room isn't bad at all!" I turned to see my mom
look around her at new home, for the time being, grinning
at how close the TV was to her bed. I rolled my eyes at her
bright mood, and knew she was doing it for me.

"So, I left all your bags with clothes and other
essentials on the right side of the couch, and on the left I
put your entertainment needs. And yes, that includes all
seasons of Supernatural," she squealed and ran over to hug
me.

"You know, the mother is traditionally supposed to take
care of her kid, not the other way around," she smiled,
pinching my cheek. I laughed and pulled her hand away.

"You've done enough mom, it's time for you to relax,"
I sighed. She gave me one of her short, sad smiles. She
looked at Kennedy and pointed her frail finger at her.

"Keep an eye on him, he tends to be a pessimistic ass,"
my mouth dropped, as Kennedy bursted out in laughter. As
if on cue, Harrison walked in with the last two duffle bags
on his back and quickly set them down by the door.

"I love you Ms. Smith, but what the hell do you have in
these bags?" Harrison exclaimed, cracking his back before
walking over to us.

"I have to keep in shape somehow, even though this
place is nice, the gym is horrible," My mom explained
simply. Harrison looked at her dumbfounded.

"So you gave me the bags with all the weights in them… on purpose?"

"You're a young boy, stop whining," We all laughed at Harrison's face once more until the nurse knocked on the door.

"Hello Ms. Smith, Dr. Carter will see you when you're ready," She gave us a sweet smile and turned the corner.

We all were kicked back into the reality of things and a collective sigh was taken, as if we all were headed into battle with premonition of what's going to happen next. My mom looked at me, and had her knuckles slightly touch my chin. "Chin up son, it'll be okay in the end."

"And if it's not okay…" I added.

"Then it's not the end," she smiled at me, trying to keep her tears in her eyes, and before letting mine fall I held onto her tightly. "Aunt Sammy will be here by tomorrow, be nice to her… and I want you here every week to tell me how it's going. Am I clear young man?" She tried to be stern and I laughed, but nodded my head. She reluctantly let go, and hugged Kennedy immediately after. She whispered something in her ear and Kennedy laughed with all her heart and smiled at my mom as she let go. Lastly, Harrison let my mom grab him into a bear hug.

"And you, don't disappear again or I will climb out of this god damn bed and get you myself," Harrison chuckled at her threat.

"I promise on Ken's life," He joked at Kennedy punched him in the shoulder. She finally let go and smiled as tears fell down her face.

"I want updates and visits. Gifts are also greatly appreciated," she laughed at her own joke and sniffled. "I love you." We all collectively said it back and waved her goodbye as she walked out and followed the nurse. I let out a breath I've been holding in and I felt Kennedy's small hand slip into mine.

No one really said anything, and honestly I was thankful for that. I didn't need anyone to say they were sorry, or that it was such a shame this happened to my family. Because my mom is still here, and I know it'll be okay. Even if it's not okay, I will be with my mom every step of the way, and I know that Kennedy and Harrison will be there too. Having people not understand what you're going through but still make the effort to try— those are the people you keep. And I'm lucky as hell to have people like that in my life. Even if I am a bullshit boy.

We all walked out of the room and turned to leave, when Kennedy tugged on my arm. I called Harrison who was walking in front of me to wait.

"Oh my god," Kennedy said. Harrison came back to us and looked over to Kennedy.

"What?"

"That girl in the heather grey sweatshirt…by the desk over there, that's Emily… Emily Parker, do you remember?" Harrison and I looked at each other, and he suddenly snapped his fingers.

"Shit, you're right. She was in our third grade class, Jason. And my Freshman english class," Harrison recalled.

"She was friends with August," Kennedy said softer, probably for Harrison's sake. We all found ourselves staring at Emily, she was sitting on a high chair, laughing at the woman behind the desk. She looked happy, glowing almost. The lady behind the desk kept on telling her to get down and go back to the main hall, but Emily just kept on fucking around. I laughed at her rambunctious attitude, it was so unlike the Emily I remembered but she looked

107

better. She was wearing a white hospital tag, and suddenly everything clicked.

"I didn't know this was where she was," Harrison said softly.

"I visited her a couple of months back... she looks better now. Much better," Kennedy added. I wasn't surprised Kennedy knew about Emily's whereabouts. Kennedy is always like that— she just knows, she just understands; always in places most are surprised to find her.

In a quick moment, Emily locked eyes with the group of weirdos staring at her. She stopped mid-sentence and immediately recognized all of us. I thought she was going to run away, and pretend she didn't see us at all. That's what the old Emily would've done.

Instead, a bright smile appeared on her face and she waved at us as if we were lost memories being found again.

Kennedy

Emily walked over to us, hopefully not feigning the confidence she seemed to have. She stopped in front of me, and I let go of Jason's hand to give her hug. I know she didn't expect me to touch her because it took her a moment to return the gesture. She squeezed me a little before letting go and smiling in my direction.

"You seem to be in happy spirits since the last time I saw you," she laughed sheepishly, probably feeling bad for the last time we spoke.

"You seem the same, maybe even better," She replied rubbing the back of her neck.

"What happened the last time?" Harrison asked behind me. Emily did a double-take as she gazed at Harrison.

"Holy fuck Harrison! What did happen? You completely got more attractive since the last time I saw you," Harrison laughed louder than he should've. "You too Jason— but the last time I saw you was in 7th grade, so I'll give you the benefit of the doubt."

"You changed too…but it suits you," Harrison added. Emily smirked at him and chuckled.

"Thanks Harrison…always a one with words," she stuffed her hands into her sweatshirt and sighed. "Well, boys what happened, before I forget to apologize, is that your little annoying angel here was the only one from the school that visited me and seemed to care. But I was a dick and pushed her away…and I also said some really shitty things. Sorry about that, I wasn't really in a good place back then," she started to explain, but I quickly cut her off.

"You don't need to explain yourself, I forgive you," I smiled. She squeezed my arm and nodded her head. "So, when are you coming back?"

"Soon actually, next month on the eighteenth," She smiled glowed with just the thought.

"That's amazing! You have to stop by, I insist," I replied with the same energy. She looked at Jason and Harrison once again, and her face filled with confusion

"It would be very touching if all of you came to see me, but I know that's not why you're all here," she stated. I shifted towards Jason, not sure if he wanted to let Emily know. Yet, he cleared his throat and reached for my hand again before answering.

"My mom was just admitted, for—," Emily put her hand up, making Jason stop mid sentence.

"Say no more, for one more month, your mother is in my care. Trust me, I know this place like the back of my hand. She will be absolutely fine here, don't you worry. I'm good at this," she gave a reassuring smile to Jason, and he reciprocated.

Suddenly, a boy with long brown hair popped out of a door behind us. "Emily! You have 3 minutes until she notices!" He scream-whispered urgently. Instead of looking scared, Emily looked excited, as if she loved a good chase.

"Well, this has been absolutely refreshing. It was really good seeing you all again, really it is. But, if I don't want to stay here any longer, I need to get back to where I'm supposed to be," she quickly pulled me into another hug, and waved back as she sprinted to the foggy door behind her, glowing with every fiber in her being.

As I thought before, I don't know if we all are destined for failure or greatness— hell I don't even know if we all are making the right choices, or if there is even something called the right choice. But all I know is that we are going out in the best way possible, and Emily seems to be headed that way. And as I walk behind Harrison and Jason making jokes about how flattered she made Harrison, while holding my Bullshit Boy's hand, I know I'm headed that way too.

Harrison

"Do I really have to do this man?" I groaned again, my hands in my pocket trying to keep them warm. He looked at me again, his face screwed up in reluctance. "It'll feel weird without it, seriously. It's just one of those things... like a good luck charm!"

"It's a fucking cigarette. That's depressing if that's your lucky charm," I replied monotoned.

"You're the one in love with Bukowski, shouldn't you take that as a metaphor or something," He huffed like the bullshit boy he is.

"Just throw it away, or smoke it," I responded wanting to get out of this cold.

"I don't want to smoke it, and I can't throw it away. That's just a waste."

"God, do you want to give it a proper funeral or something?" I joked and he glared at me as if what I said was too harsh. "You know, even if you seem like a hard-ass, you're cheesy as fuck."

"I could say the same thing to you," he replied without missing a beat. The bright orange color burned up the sky and allowed no clouds to pass. If it wasn't so damn cold, I would stay a bit longer. After convincing Coach (for about three damn hours) to let Jason back on the team, I told him there was no longer a reason to keep the cigarette I gave him. Although, I didn't know he'd taken a liking to it. He kept on twirling the cigarette in his hands and kept staring at the sky as if there was a secret answer up there.

"How's your mom?" I asked suddenly.

"Good, she's getting chemo, and it seems to be working. She also is raving about how many channels her TV has, so that's always a good thing," he chuckled slightly. A silence settled between us, and usually it wasn't so awkward until I could feel what he wanted to ask me. I appreciated that he didn't mention her name, and he probably knew how I would probably flip like a switch if he even said it. I think he knew that eventually, I will have to talk about it. But for now, I have to keep staring at the sky. Maybe there is an answer in there somewhere.

"Remember that time at the run down barn?" Jason started laughing suddenly with the very thought of the memory.

"Holy shit, yea," I mimicked his happy nature and I found myself clutching my stomach.

"I still can't believe I did that in front of all of them," Jason shook his head, just like every time he remembered his embarrassing memory.

"That was when you still had a crush on Jenn from Chicago," I added.

"I was a fucking idiot," he wiped his eyes, calming down. "She moved back to Chicago."

We laughed quietly again, nostalgia running through our veins. "That was a long time ago," I whispered.

"Yea, still scarring though," He said, sighing. "I wonder if she ever wrote that book she kept on talking about?"

"Oh yea, or either applied to that college she never stopped talking about…," I chuckled. He slowly nodded his head, flicking the cigarette slower now.

"You shouldn't worry about that now though. Maybe in five years time we'll go up to Chicago and see where Jenn ends up. Just out of curiosity…" I knew he didn't give a fuck about Jenn from Chicago, but I knew what he did care about. I knew what was bothering him, and he knew what was bothering me. It's like this silent language no one really has to make known— its like it's always there. You just have to feel it.

I looked up at the sky one more time, and sighed as I pulled away from the orange cascade. I took the lighter that was in his hands, and burnt the cigarette until only the nub was left. I shoved him with my shoulder and started to walk ahead.

"Let's go home bullshit boy," I heard him cuss at me, but his footsteps trailed behind.

For some reason I felt a small weight lift off my chest as I buried my hands deeper into my jacket pockets. A sense of acceptance came with the wind.

I don't know what decisions I made will eventually become consequences in the future. In other words I don't know what the fuck is going to happen. I'm just going to take it day by day, stomping out each cigarette I see. And even though there no certainty of my greatness, or any greatness in general, I felt Jason run up by my side as the sight of my house came into vision, and I thought of her. And somehow I knew, I can't tell how, but I knew, we'll be okay.

Pluto

...

Acknowledgments

I want to thank my family, and my lost souls for believing in me and always being there. This novella means a lot to me and it makes me beyond grateful for all the people taking their time to read it and fall in love with the characters as I had. Thank you to all my friends who helped me throughout this writing experience. Especially Rebecca Reilly, I couldn't have done this without you. Thank you for all the support and liking the cheesiness of this novella. Thank you to Michael Howard for the absolutely beautiful cover.

Thank you to my publisher. Thank you to my (many) editors.

I hope we all someday learn the art of being here.

your small planet friend,

p.

About the Author

Ileena '*Pluto*' Irving is a 17 year old girl living in a small town in New Jersey. She has been writing since she was in 4th grade and started to self-publish once she turned 15. She published a story on Wattpad that reached 1.8 million reads, and she also has a very successful poetic twitter account that has a substantial amount of followers. In August of 2015 she published her first poetry book *To You, Him, and Everyone Else,* available on iBooks and Amazon. This novella is her second publication. She wants to give thanks to Michael Howard for the beautiful cover, and to the many people who helped edit this book.

CPSIA information can be obtained
at www.ICGtesting.com
Printed in the USA
FSHW020749240119
55230FS